"Dance with me," Kelly said softly, and Jo was powerless to refuse. She moved into her arms eagerly, refusing to think about what she was inviting. Kelly held her tightly, both arms behind Johanna's back as Jo slid her arms over Kelly's shoulders, pulling her close. They danced together slowly, feet barely moving, bodies pressed together. Jo closed her eyes and let the music wash over her, breathing deeply as she smelled the perfume at Kelly's neck. Her lips pressed there before she knew what she was doing, and she heard Kelly's sharp intake of breath, felt her arms tighten around her. It was the rum, she reasoned. Why else would she be acting so wantonly? Kelly moved her head, and her lips found Jo's in an instant. Her own mouth opened. Feeling the tip of Kelly's tongue, she thought her knees would buckle from desire. Her own tongue found its way into Kelly's mouth, and she moaned deep in her throat, forgetting the other couples dancing around them. Kelly pulled her into a dark corner in the back and pressed her against the wall, her hand boldly cupping Jo's breast. Jo leaned into her, her nipples hard and sensitive to Kelly's touch. Their kiss was hungry, passionate, tongues dancing, desire growing.

"I want you," Kelly whispered into her mouth.

"Yes," Jo agreed. God, how she wanted her, too.

"Let's get out of here."

One Summer Night

GERRI HILL

2004

Bella Books, Inc.
P.O. Box 10543
Tallahassee, FL 32302

Printed in the United States of America on acid-free paper.

First Published 2000 by Rising Tide Press
First Edition

Cover designer: Sandy Knowles

ISBN 1-59493-007-4

Acknowledgements

I started writing *One Summer Night* in June of 1994. And it *was* hot, especially after having spent the last few years in the mountains of Colorado! The softball team is a tribute to the city league team I labored on every Monday and Thursday night (when I was much younger!). Bev, the pitcher, was the leader, but I'm not sure if it was because she was the pitcher or because her mother owned a beer joint at the edge of town. The locals all raised their eyebrows when the team came to visit! Thanks to all those gals who made playing ball so much fun, especially Lori, who liked her women "sporty" and not "fluffy"!

I also want to thank Bella Books and Linda Hill for considering publishing *One Summer Night*, and thanks to those of you who have enough interest to pick it up again.

Also, a quick thank you to Stephanie Solomon, queen of Academy of Bards, who has been "itching" to get her hands on *One Summer Night* for years! And thanks, too, to my good friend, Marquita, (whose husband will die to know this!), who found Kelly Sambino to be "hot"!

I hope you all enjoy this, my first attempt at writing a little romance.

About the Author

Gerri lives in the Piney Woods of East Texas with her partner, Diane, and their two labs, Zach and Max. The resident cats Sierra, Tori and now Jordan, round out the household. Hobbies include any outdoor activity, from tending the orchard and vegetable garden to hiking in the woods with camera and binoculars. For more, visit Gerri's website at: www.gerrihill.com

Chapter One

It was hot. Much too hot for June, she thought, as she pointed the air conditioning vent toward her face and sped down MoPac in her new black Mazda. Peering out the sunroof she saw nothing but blue skies, not even one puffy white cloud to shield the sun. She grimaced. Summer in Austin had hit with a bang.

Again she wondered why she had let herself be talked into going to the softball tournament. Betsy, her best friend, had been calling all week asking her to come until she had finally relented. Summer was her time. Her time to be alone and catch up on all the things she had missed during the year. With no classes to teach until the fall semester, she wanted to spend the summer going to Lake Travis when the mood hit and catching up on her reading, not sitting in the hot sun watching women run around the bases. But Betsy had argued that if she was ever to meet anyone, she had to get out. Well, Johanna Marshall didn't want to meet anyone, she stubbornly insisted, but Betsy wouldn't hear of it.

"You're only thirty-six. My God, you're acting as if your life is over and you've resigned yourself to being an old maid.

"I'm not an old maid. I'm just not interested in a relationship right now," she told her.

"Who's talking relationship? You never go out, Jo. I hate to think of you always being by yourself. It's been three years, you know."

"I'm well aware of how long it's been."

"Then come out with us. We'll drink a few beers and cheer them on."

So, she had agreed finally. After all, it *had* been over three years since Nancy left her to return to New York. A job transfer, she had said. Johanna laughed bitterly to herself. Three years had not squelched her anger. When she found out Nancy had been secretly seeing someone else for nearly six months before she and her new girlfriend had both up and moved, Johanna had been devastated. How could she have been so blind that she hadn't noticed? Had she grown so complacent in their relationship that it just never occurred to her that Nancy had become distant? That Nancy had another lover? They had spent four years together, the last two sharing Jo's house on Bull Creek, and she had been naive enough to think things were perfect between them.

She shook her head, not wanting to dredge up those old memories. Instead, she concentrated on driving, hands tight on the wheel as Saturday traffic zoomed by around her. She was still protective of her new car, and had not yet reverted to her usual habit of cutting in and out of traffic. Spotting her exit, she was soon just a few blocks from the large complex of ball fields in South Austin. An acre of cars filled the parking area. Johanna remembered Betsy had said it was the largest women's tournament Austin had ever hosted. Teams from all over Texas, as well as a few from other states, were there.

She finally found a parking space on the back row and opened her door to the heat. She scowled again. Summer in Austin was not her favorite time of year. Oh, she loved going to the lake and floating in her tube on Bull Creek, but each year the summers seemed to last longer and longer. She was thankful she had worn a tank top. The slight breeze was not helping much. She pulled the top away from her breasts, fanning cool air inside. She rarely wore a bra, one benefit to being small-breasted, she thought. Probably the only benefit. Taking her lawn chair and her small cooler of beer from the trunk, she walked to the fields.

There were ten softball fields here. She headed to field number three, where their team was playing. She spotted Betsy and Janis and made her way through the crowd to them, excusing herself as she bumped into people with her chair and cooler.

"You came!" Betsy exclaimed, standing up and making room for her.

"I told you I would," Johanna said, forcing a smile. She was already crabby as she felt sweat trickle between her shoulder blades.

"Yes, but you're late. It started a half hour ago."

Johanna shrugged, opened her chair and shoved her cooler under it. "Hello, Janis. Hot enough for you?"

Janis laughed at Jo's usual comment and introduced her to the others sitting with them.

"This is Kerry and Shea," she said, pointing to two older women sitting next to her. "I'm sure you've heard me mention them."

"Yes," Jo said and smiled.

"And that's Lucy." She motioned toward a younger woman who looked up and smiled, then turned her attention back to the game.

"Lucy works with Deb," Janis explained.

"I haven't seen Deb in ages," she said, plopping unceremoniously into her chair, her eyes closed against the heat. "God, I could be sitting in the water right now," she murmured.

"Oh, give me a break," Betsy said. "It's not that hot."

"Ninety-five and June's not even half over. What's August going to be like?"

"One hundred, like always," she said. Reaching under Johanna's chair, she took a beer from the ice and handed it to her. "Here, cool off."

"Thanks." Jo twisted the top off the bottle, drank nearly half of it, then rubbed the cold bottle on her face. "Oh, that's so good, " she sighed.

"Yeah."

"So, what's the score?" she asked.

"We're up by one," Janis replied and yelled at Cindy to get a hit.

Betsy and Janis had never played softball. In fact, Jo doubted Janis had ever played any sport. Nevertheless, they made every softball game, and Betsy jokingly referred to themselves as the team's mascot. They made an odd duo. Janis, short and pudgy. Betsy, tall and thin, with a head full of red curls. But they were the happiest couple Jo had ever met, still going strong after thirteen years.

Jo turned her attention to the game. She knew nearly everyone on the team. Not that she made that many games, but they had been playing together for years, and since they were all friends of Betsy's, she had been out with them before. A few of the regular members couldn't make the tournament, and Jo knew Christy had come in from San Antonio to play.

"Is Kay playing?" Johanna asked. Kay was a friend of hers from college who she had introduced to Betsy years ago.

"She's playing second today," Betsy said. "Christy brought someone along with her from San Antonio to play third."

Christy was Betsy's cousin and, despite that, they were good friends. Betsy looked at her and frowned. "Didn't you bring a cap?"

"No," she said, squinting her blue eyes against the sun. "I left without sunscreen, too. Do you have any?"

"I do," Janis offered, reaching into her bag for the sunblock. "God, it's hell getting old. Isn't it?"

Johanna flicked her a wry glance and opened the tube.

"I mean, remember when we would stay out for hours and not even think about wrinkles?"

"Skin cancer, Janis," Jo told her. "Not wrinkles."

"There was no such thing as sunscreen when we were young. I'm sure the damage is already done."

"What do you mean, when we were young?" Betsy asked with a laugh.

"I'm nearly forty, if you'll remember. My days of youth are past."

"You've been nearly forty for three years," Jo teased.

"Yeah, well, this time, it's for real," she said.

Betsy winked at Johanna. "Three more months," she said quietly. "That's how long we'll have to listen to it."

Cindy smacked a fly ball out to center field and the inning was over. Jo spotted Kay as she headed to second base and waved at her.

"I haven't seen Kay in a while," she said.

"Well, if you would come out with us more, you would," Betsy retorted.

"You know I don't go to the bar during the semester."

"Everyone knows you're gay. What's the big deal?"

"I just would hate to run into one of my students there."

The players ran to their positions, and her eyes followed a woman she didn't know. The woman was tall and lean and very tan. Jo watched as she jogged to third base. Pulling her cap off, the stranger ran her fingers through her short, dark hair, brushing it away from her face. She was very dark, one of those people who had a tan no matter what time of year it was, one of those people Johanna had always been jealous of. She had to work at her tan, being so blonde and blue-eyed.

The woman pulled the cap back on her head and kicked dirt with her foot. She pounded her glove with her hand, and then crouched in the ready position while Johanna stared at her. God, she's cute, she thought.

"That's Kelly Sambino," Betsy said, following her gaze.

"Who?" Jo asked innocently.

"Third base."

"Oh." She pulled her eyes away, embarrassed. She had never been one to stare.

Sharon, the pitcher, was the youngest member of the team, not yet thirty, and she turned around, making sure her teammates were ready before tossing the first pitch. Johanna watched as it sailed high, then slid her eyes back to third base. The woman yelled something to Sharon, then moved in a little closer on the infield. The next pitch was hit high to the outfield, and the left fielder moved under it, caught it effortlessly and then threw it back to the infield.

Johanna sat back in her chair to watch Sharon pitch but couldn't keep her gaze off third for long. Her eyes followed the ball bouncing up the third base line. Kelly Sambino charged it, picked it up smoothly and fired it to first base. The runner was out by three steps. Jo smiled as Kelly turned and walked back to third base. The next hitter flied out, and Jo's eyes followed the dark woman as she jogged back to the dugout, accepting congratulations from her teammates.

Johanna couldn't see her in the dugout so she purposely kept her eyes on the field. Kay was the first to bat, and Jo cheered her on when the first pitch was hit over the shortstop's head into the outfield. Then her breath caught as Kelly Sambino walked confidently to the plate, taking a few practice swings before stepping into the batter's box.

"Come on, Kelly," Kay yelled from first base.

"She hit a home run her first time up," Janis said.

"Really?" Jo murmured, trying to sound nonchalant, all the while watching intently as Kelly waited for the first pitch. It was low, and she stepped back and took another practice swing. Johanna saw the muscles in Kelly's arms stand out as she clutched the bat. She strained to hear as Kelly spoke to the catcher, smiling briefly before turning her attention back to the pitcher. The next pitch was perfect, and Kelly sent it flying to the outfield. The left fielder turned and ran toward the fence but the ball sailed over her head. Kay was already rounding third. Kelly ran past second base and raced for third, diving headfirst to the bag, just beating the throw.

Jo found herself cheering along with the rest of the crowd, watching with interest as Kelly stood up and dusted off her pants and shirt, her hands moving over her breasts and stomach absently as she grinned, teeth white against her tan. Johanna stared at her, unable to look away as Kelly chatted with the player from the other team, all the while a smile firmly in place, as if she was surprised at her hit.

"She's quite a player," Betsy said. "Christy said she used to play college ball in California."

Jo nodded and again forced herself to look away. It was becoming embarrassing, the way she was staring. It was so unlike her to have such an instant attraction to someone, especially someone she had yet to meet. Besides, she doubted she would even like her. Women like her had girls falling over them all the time. Kelly probably had a string of women littering the streets of San Antonio at this very moment.

The next two batters struck out, and Kelly still stood at third, clapping her hands, urging Deb to bring her home. Deb hit the first pitch, and it rolled between first and second, just out of the other team's reach, and Kelly trotted home, stepped on the plate and picked up Deb's discarded bat.

"Way to go, Sambino," someone yelled from the dugout, and Jo watched as Kelly walked in front of them, still smiling. For a second, she looked their way. Jo froze as dark eyes settled on her briefly. Then Kelly went into the dugout, accepting handslaps from her teammates, now out of Jo's view, who turned her attention, with effort, back to the field.

The game ended twenty minutes later, and Jo stood to stretch her legs. The heat she hadn't even thought about during the game now settled around her again. Grabbing another beer from her cooler, she took a long swallow and wiped her brow. The teams were on the field shaking hands and talking. She forced her eyes away from Kelly Sambino and settled them on Kay, who was walking toward the fence.

"Jo! Glad you came," Kay called.

"Hi. You had a good game, Kay."

"Thanks. We've got another one at three. Are you staying?"

"Yes," she said immediately.

"Good. I'll talk to you in a minute," Kay said and walked to the dugout.

Jo waved at Deb as she walked back to the dugout and realized that she had not spoken to Deb since Christmas. Or was it New Year's? They had been good friends once, sharing meals and movies. When they had both been single, they'd spent many an evening together. But then Jo had started seeing Nancy and Deb had disappeared from her life, except for group holidays, it seemed. She sighed. Wasn't that how it always was? Give up your friends for a lover, and when the lover leaves, your friends are gone, too. Jo sighed again. It was as if they were strangers now, and Jo made a mental note to invite her to dinner some night soon.

Feeling a tap on her shoulder, she realized where she was, looked away from the field, and followed Betsy and Janis as they went to meet the players. Johanna was acutely aware of her nervousness as her eyes searched for Kelly Sambino. She spotted her talking to Christy and knew that Betsy and Janis were heading that way. She briefly hung back, almost afraid to meet her, but Betsy turned around and motioned for her to follow.

"Are you kidding? I was lucky to make it to third," Kelly was saying to Christy with a smile, and Jo caught her breath as Kelly looked around and rested those dark eyes on her again.

"Great game!" Betsy applauded. "A shutout."

"Yeah. They were picked to win the tournament, too," Christy grinned. She turned to Johanna then. "Jo, this is Kelly Sambino, a friend of mine from San Antonio." She turned to Kelly and pointed at Jo. "Johanna Marshall."

"Hi," Kelly said and stuck out her hand.

Jo was forced to take it, to feel Kelly's fingers wrap around her hand, to feel her firm grip. She kept her eyes down as their hands clasped, then raised them to meet Kelly's deep brown eyes directly.

"Nice to meet you. You had a good game," she said.

Kelly released her hand slowly and smiled. "Thanks, but those were lucky hits. My softball days ended years ago."

"Oh, please," Christy groaned. "I had to practically beg her to play and look what she does."

Kelly grinned, showing off even, white teeth. "It's been a lot of years, Christy."

"You're far from the oldest one on this team."

"I think you hold that honor, don't you?" Betsy asked, and they all laughed.

"And you're not too far behind me, cousin," Christy shot back.

Jo smiled and raised her eyes again, only to find Kelly Sambino looking at her. She met her eyes briefly, and then looked away, back toward the field where another team was warming up.

"I've got to get something to drink," Kelly said, and to Johanna, "Listen, it was nice to meet you. I hope you hang around for the next game."

"I will," she said and smiled.

"Good." Kelly turned to the others. "See you later," she said and left them.

"She's good, Christy," Janis commented, when Kelly had walked off. "Where did you find her?"

"She teaches at St. Peter's. Well, for the last year anyway. She's from California originally and used to play for Stanford when she was in college."

"So where did you meet her?" Betsy asked.

"Out at a party awhile back. She's very nice. I really like her."

Jo listened to the conversation, her eyes following Kelly Sambino as she walked toward the parking lot. She was intrigued with her, to say the least. Actually, infatuated would be a better word.

They stood in the shade, visiting, and Jo was glad she had come. Kay came over to catch up, as they had not seen each other in a couple of months. She also got reacquainted with the other players she hadn't seen in awhile, but she couldn't keep herself from scanning the parking lot for Kelly, waiting for her return.

"Jo?"

Jo turned around and smiled at Deb, giving her a quick hug in greeting.

"It's been so long, Deb. How are you?"

"I'm good. You?"

"Fine," she said. "We haven't seen each other in ages. Why did we let that happen?"

"Well, we just sort of lost touch when you started dating Nancy," Deb said, "and never seemed to connect again after you two broke up."

"It was my fault," Jo agreed. "Why don't we have dinner some night? Or is that not a good idea?" Jo looked around to see if someone were watching them. "Are you seeing someone?"

"No, no. You know me, always single," Deb reassured her. "Dinner sounds good."

"Terrific. We'll get together and catch up," Jo said.

Deb left her and Jo turned around, looking for Betsy, but aware that she was searching for Kelly Sambino, as well. Oh, she was acting like a teenager with a huge crush. She purposefully strode back to her lawn chair, thinking she really did need to get out more.

Kelly did not reappear until just before the start of the next game. The others were already warming up when she hurried on to the field, carrying her bat and glove and a bottle of water.

Despite telling herself how foolish she was being, Jo watched closely. She stared as Kelly picked up a ball and began throwing with Christy, her lean body angling into every throw. She smiled often and chatted with the player next to her as she absently tossed the softball back and forth. Jo was mesmerized. She couldn't tear her eyes away.

"Hey," Betsy said to her, bringing her around.

"Yeah?"

"What are you looking at?" she asked with a smile.

Jo blushed and cursed silently to herself. "Nothing."

"Yeah," she said, punching her arm. "Nice to know something's still alive in there."

Jo ignored her and took another beer from her cooler. Their team was in the third base dugout this time and although she had a perfect view of the bench, she purposely refrained from staring. Instead, she pretended interest in the other team as they warmed up, trying to find someone to hold her attention as Kelly Sambino had done. No one did.

The game started, and her eyes never traveled far from third base. Kelly played her position expertly, grabbing every ground ball that came her way and throwing a bullet to first base each time. Jo was impressed, to say the least. But it was Kelly's hitting that won the game. Her first time up, with two runners on, she smashed the ball to center field, and Jo smiled as it sailed to the fence. Then she watched as Kelly ran the bases, her long legs gracefully touching each one as she hurried to home before the ball ever made it back to the infield.

Kelly's grin was huge and contagious as she crossed home plate and hit hands with the others who had crossed in front of her. Jo watched her with awe all the way to the dugout.

"Wow!" Janis exclaimed.

"Yeah," Betsy agreed.

After it was over, Johanna stood with the others as they talked about the game, going over each play again. Kelly seemed embarrassed at the attention she was getting and once again attributed her hits to sheer luck. Jo was secretly pleased that someone with her obvious talent wasn't conceited or arrogant about it. Then again, maybe if she was a little more stuck-up, it would quell this attraction Jo was feeling for Kelly Sambino.

Everyone was deciding to go for Mexican food, and Jo found herself agreeing to dinner before she even realized it.

"Don't be late this time, Jo," Betsy admonished as they were leaving.

"I won't." She closed her trunk with a bang and settled inside her car, turning the air conditioning on high as she drove home. She refused to acknowledge that she had agreed to dinner simply because Kelly Sambino was going to be there. It was high time she went out. Like Betsy keeps saying. Right! With that, she shoved a CD in and listened to Elton John on her way home.

Chapter Two

Of course she was late. After her shower, she couldn't decide what to wear. It was still so hot out, she couldn't see putting on jeans, but then shorts seemed too casual. After ironing both and laying them on the bed, she decided on the jeans anyway. Tucking in a crisp cotton shirt, refusing to speculate on the extra effort she was making with her appearance, she carefully applied the minimal amount of makeup she normally wore and sprayed perfume lightly on her neck and wrists. Her blonde hair was cut short for the summer and she brushed it away from her face with a few quick strokes.

She stared in the mirror longer than usual. She had been in the sun too long and her cheeks showed it. Peering closer, she rubbed a finger lightly under one eye. Wrinkles! They were starting to show and she stepped back. They were not nearly as evident from this distance. Laughing at herself, she put her hands on her hips and threw back her shoulders, hoping it made her look taller. It didn't. She wasn't really short. She just wasn't tall. She had spent her high school years wishing she were short and petite so that the guys would notice her more. Then she had spent her college years wishing she were taller, especially after she had developed her first crush on a woman, a basketball player, no less! But she was the same average, boring, and middle-of-the-pack size she had been since she turned seventeen. She gave her hair one last brush with her fingers and hurried out.

They had agreed to meet at Bonita's Cafe on Congress Avenue at seven o'clock, and it was already fifteen past when Johanna drove by slowly, looking for a parking spot. After cruising by twice, she finally parked two blocks away and hurried along the sidewalk, spotting Betsy's car only a few spaces from the front door. Some people have all the luck, she thought.

She heard them before she actually saw them. Before the hostess could ask her, she simply smiled, pointed and made her way through the crowd waiting for tables.

"Jo, I thought maybe you had decided not to come," Betsy said. She had saved a place next to her and motioned for her to sit. Johanna thankfully sat down, saying hello to those around her.

"Running late, as usual," she murmured.

"Well, I ordered you a margarita. I hope that's okay."

"That's fine," she said, smiling her thanks. Only then did she look around the table. Most of the players and their girlfriends were there, and Jo knew most of them. Her eyes stopped when they met the glittering dark ones of Kelly Sambino. Kelly smiled at her from across the table, holding her gaze, and Jo felt the heat she thought she had left outside. She flushed and looked away, grabbing the glass of water in front of her. She took a long swallow, avoiding the gaze from across the table.

Her margarita came, and Jo sipped gratefully, feeling the coolness of it slide down her throat. It was just hot out, she told herself. She had been in the sun too long! She ordered her usual enchilada dinner, then munched on the warm tortilla chips and salsa that were placed within her reach. The conversation around the table centered on the games, and as they enthusiastically rehashed every play and every hit, Jo listened, all the while conscious of the woman sitting across from her. As Kelly told about her hits, how she had just lucked into the home runs, Jo was able to observe her. Her long, slim fingers held her glass lightly, and she absently rubbed the frost from the side as she spoke. She seemed almost embarrassed about the attention she was getting. Jo noticed how she quickly turned the conversation to Sharon, who had pitched two shutout games.

"Oh, like I didn't have help behind me," Sharon said. She was sitting next to Mattie, who Jo had only met once before.

"Let's face it, we've got a good team," Deb said, and they all agreed.

Johanna was silent through most of the meal, but she missed little, least of all Kelly Sambino. She watched her constantly when she wasn't looking, lowering her eyes quickly whenever Kelly glanced her way. She spoke quietly to Betsy and Janis, but didn't take part in the conversation around the table. She wasn't quite certain what to make of her attraction to Kelly. It was so out of character for her that she attributed it to the heat of summer. Why else would she be staring at a virtual stranger, wondering if brown eyes could really be that dark?

After dinner, they stood on the street, the air having cooled to a tolerable seventy-five degrees. No one was ready to end the evening, and as they stood around talking, Sharon suggested they go dancing.

"Lakers has country music or we could go to Uptown," she said.

She was met with groans from the older ones. "Uptown is filled with college students," Janis said.

"Okay, then Lakers. It's still early. Our game isn't until nine tomorrow."

They agreed, and before Johanna could offer a protest, they were splitting up, each hurrying to their cars. She paused beside Betsy's car, watching as Kelly got into Christy's van.

"I won't stay long," she told Betsy pointedly.

"Of course not," Betsy agreed with a smile.

"Really. I'm only going for one drink."

"Okay. Sure." Betsy and Janis both grinned at her.

"You can wipe those smiles off your faces, too," she called over her shoulder as she walked toward her car. So, she was infatuated with the woman. Big deal! After three years, she was happy to know that that part of her was apparently coming back to life. It wasn't as if she was going to do anything about it. But still, she wondered if Kelly might ask her to dance. Then she wondered if she would allow herself to accept.

She slammed her door and locked it, then turned the AC on high. Sitting there for a moment, she caught a glimpse of her bright eyes in the mirror and attributed it to the margarita, nothing else. Hell, for all she knew, Christy and Kelly could be seeing each other. But she doubted it. Christy had been living with the same woman for years now and was very happy. But then again, Johanna would have said the same thing about herself only three years ago.

She drove the few blocks to the downtown bar and found a parking space easily, as it was barely nine and the regular Saturday night crowd had not yet arrived. Betsy and Janis were waiting for her at the entrance. Each paid the cover charge and walked into the dark bar. It was already smoky, but thankfully cool. Loud country music blared from the speakers. They had pulled several tables together, and once again, Jo found herself sitting across from Kelly, who already was sipping a drink.

"What'll you have?" Betsy asked.

"Rum and coke, please," Jo answered, and Betsy left to get their drinks.

"Betsy says you rarely come out with them," Christy said from across the table.

"Rarely," Jo said and smiled. "I'm too busy during the regular terms."

"Kelly teaches also," Christy said. "Though this may be her last year. She's got a novel published and it's due out this fall."

"Really? What do you teach?" Jo asked, looking at Kelly directly for the first time but avoiding the dark eyes that tried to capture hers.

Kelly gave her an amused smile. "Journalism."

"Giving that up to write books? God, who could blame you," Johanna said and grinned.

"I really enjoy teaching, but it leaves me little time to write."

"What kind of book?"

"It's a murder mystery. Takes place on a college campus. What else?" she laughed.

"I can think of several professors at my own campus who would be candidates for either the victim or the villain," Jo said and smiled at her.

"Really? Maybe you should try your own. It's great therapy," Kelly said. "Especially if your dean won't cooperate with you." She leaned forward, placed elbows on the table, and Jo did the same. "What do you teach?"

"English," Jo admitted, suddenly feeling like the frumpy old professor that Betsy claimed she was evolving into. "And composition," she added, as if that sounded a little more glamorous.

Betsy came back with their drinks, then pulled Janis up to dance. Jo sipped hers, then looked back at Kelly. "You're from California?"

"Yes. San Francisco."

"What brought you here?" Jo asked.

"The teaching position. It was something different. But mostly, I wanted to see what a real summer was like."

"And what do you think?"

She laughed. "I'm wondering how I've survived two of them. No wonder the lakes are so popular around here."

Betsy and Janis came back as a very old Anne Murray song came on and Kelly looked at Jo and smiled. "I'm not much for country music but I think I can manage this song. Would you like to dance?"

Johanna hesitated, her drink halfway to her mouth. She set it back down. "Okay."

Jo walked around the table and Kelly took her hand, leading her to the dance floor. Their eyes met before Jo lightly laid her hand on Kelly's shoulder. Though they danced with nearly a foot of space between them, they moved together gracefully, as if they had done this hundreds of times before. They didn't speak, and Jo avoided looking at her. Instead, she watched the other couples around them, all dancing much closer than they were. When the song ended, they pulled apart and again their eyes met.

"Thanks," Kelly said quietly, and led her back to the table.

She met Betsy's amused glance with a scowl and ignored her as best she could. Kelly then danced with Christy, and Jo watched as they moved on the floor, noting that Kelly held her with the same distance between them as she had with Jo. That pleased her, though she didn't speculate as to why.

Conversation was sparse around the table. They were too many to talk comfortably, and the music was too loud to hear anything from the other end of the table. She was very aware of Kelly sitting across from her, daring to meet her eyes from time to time, answering her soft smile with one of her own. Kelly did not ask her to dance again until another slow song came on. Jo accepted with a smile, laid her hand in Kelly's outstretched one and followed her to the dance floor.

Kelly held her closer this time, but still there was a space between them, and Jo found herself wishing she would hold her tighter. Jo closed her eyes, letting her palm lay flat on Kelly's strong shoulder. They danced slowly, their feet moving together effortlessly, and Jo took a breath, smelling the light, fresh perfume that Kelly wore. When the song ended, they moved apart slowly, their eyes holding for a long moment before Kelly smiled.

"We dance pretty well together, don't you think?"

Smiling, Jo nodded and followed her back to the table.

Johanna accepted the new drink Betsy had bought for her. "Are you trying to prove a point?" she asked, still smiling, well aware she was past the one drink she had said she would stay for.

"You just looked thirsty from all that dancing," Betsy said pointedly.

Jo ignored her and turned away. So much for best friends. She looked up and found Kelly watching her. Their eyes held again. Jo finally looked away, flushed. She was not used to this, this sexual attraction for a stranger. Giving herself a little mental shake, she silently scolded, "Summer nights! It's just the summer heat."

She felt a tap on her shoulder, roused herself and looked up at Christy.

"How about a dance?"

"Sure."

It was a fast two-step, and they moved together well, spinning around the floor. Winded and thirsty when they returned to the table, she downed her drink.

"Another?" Betsy asked.

"No, thank you," she said. "I'll wait."

Betsy laughed and patted her shoulder. "You're such fun to tease, Jo."

"Obviously," she said dryly.

But she was having fun. Maybe Betsy was right. Maybe she did need to get out more.

When another slow love song came on, Jo bravely raised her eyes across the table, and Kelly was there, silently asking her to dance with an arch of one dark brow. Jo nodded and stood. She was aware of Betsy watching them, but no longer cared. She was having fun. She was feeling again.

This time, when they moved together, Kelly held her close, their bodies brushing, touching. She let her hand move behind Kelly's neck, ignoring the pounding of her heart. Her breath caught when Kelly's hand moved lower on her back, turning her expertly around the floor. The song ended all too soon, and they stood there, still in each other's arms, neither wanting to move away. Kelly's brown eyes were very dark as they looked into Jo's, and she continued to hold her hand as they made their way back.

This time, she accepted the drink from Betsy thankfully. She was hot and it had nothing to do with the weather, she thought with a smile. The bar had filled up. Quite a few players from other teams there now.

"Crowded tonight," she said commented.

"Yeah, there's lots of women in town," Janis agreed.

Jo nodded and watched the dance floor, now filled with couples doing the Cotton-Eyed Joe. She was thankful no one had dragged her out for that one. A fast line dance was next and she watched with amazement as everyone turned and stepped in unison, the strangers mixed with the locals. She had never gotten the hang of line dancing, maybe because she rarely tried. Nancy had seldom agreed to go dancing, even though Johanna enjoyed it. Then, after Nancy left, Jo had isolated herself. She could count on one hand the number of times she had come here since.

Kelly was watching her, she knew, but she didn't look up. She didn't trust herself. She was much too aware of her as it was. Staring into those dark eyes was too much of a temptation. However, when the next song started, she couldn't resist looking up.

"Come on," Kelly said, motioning to the floor.

Jo locked eyes with her and stood, reaching for her hand. They moved together quickly, their bodies pressed close together, Kelly's heart beating against her breasts. She clenched her jaw and closed her eyes, her hand moving into Kelly's hair. Oh, dear Lord, she thought. What am I doing? This is a perfect stranger!

Kelly's hand moved low on her back, pressing her closer, and as their hips came together, Jo couldn't suppress a low moan. Their flushed cheeks touched, and as she felt Kelly's lips graze her ear, Jo involuntarily pulled her closer. Her feet moved with a will of their own, her thoughts on anything but dancing. The dance floor was dark, masking their movements. When they were in the back, Kelly pulled away, staring at her. This time, Jo didn't look away. She watched Kelly's gaze drop to her lips, and her heart hammered in her chest as Kelly slowly brought her eyes back to Jo's. Jo watched in anticipation as Kelly's lips came closer. She closed her eyes, waiting for the kiss, wanting her kiss.

Even so, she wasn't prepared for the rush of desire that consumed her when Kelly's lips finally touched hers. Her mouth opened eagerly under Kelly's, and her feet stopped moving entirely, unable to continue their meaningless motion when all she wanted was for their kiss to continue.

Kelly drew her lips away slowly and continued their dance, forcing Jo to move with her around the floor. Kelly's arms held her tightly, and Jo was thankful, certain that she would collapse right there without them. They didn't speak when the song ended, but their hands remained locked as Kelly led her through the crowd toward their table.

Jo's eyes darted to Betsy and Janis, feeling certain that they had seen them kissing, but they were talking to Christy across the table, and no one seemed to have noticed. Flustered, she sipped her drink, refusing to look across the table at Kelly. My God, what have you done? Kissing a total stranger right on the dance floor! She downed her drink, letting the rum wash through her. If it wasn't the heat, it was the alcohol, she decided. Three drinks were one past her limit. She twirled the ice in her glass, drinking the melted water. Closing her eyes, she tried to fight the attraction she felt for Kelly Sambino and failed miserably. She looked up to find Kelly watching her, and Kelly raised her brows, giving her a small, gentle smile. Jo didn't return it. She was too embarrassed. Did Kelly think she did this sort of thing all the time? That she was used to picking up strangers in a bar? Oh, Lord, if she only knew how out of character this really was!

A slow Trisha Yearwood song started and, with a will of their own, her eyes sought Kelly.

"Dance with me," Kelly said softly, and Jo was powerless to refuse. She moved into her arms eagerly, refusing to think about what she was inviting. Kelly held her tightly, both arms behind Johanna's back as Jo slid her arms over Kelly's shoulders, pulling her close. They danced together slowly, feet barely moving, bodies pressed together. Jo closed her eyes and let the music wash over her, breathing deeply as she smelled the perfume at Kelly's neck. Her lips pressed there before she knew what she was doing, and she heard Kelly's sharp intake of breath, felt her arms tighten around her. It was the rum, she reasoned. Why else would she be acting so wantonly? Kelly moved her head, and her lips found Jo's in an instant. Her own mouth opened. Feeling the tip of Kelly's tongue, she thought her knees would buckle from desire. Her own tongue found its way into Kelly's mouth, and she moaned deep in her throat, forgetting the other couples dancing around them. Kelly pulled her into a dark corner in the back and pressed her against the wall, her hand boldly cupping Jo's breast. Jo leaned into her, her nipples hard and sensitive to Kelly's touch. Their kiss was hungry, passionate, tongues dancing, desire growing.

"I want you," Kelly whispered into her mouth.

"Yes," Jo agreed. God, how she wanted her, too.

"Let's get out of here."

Jo was too drugged with desire to offer a protest, and she nodded. She blindly followed Kelly to their table.

"Johanna is leaving, so she's going to give me a lift to the hotel," Kelly told Christy.

"So soon?" Betsy asked sweetly.

Jo met her eyes, sure she was blushing, and forced a smile anyway. "It's been a long day," was all she said.

They left quickly. Kelly followed Jo to her car. They didn't say anything on the way to Jo's house, and she was glad. She wasn't sure she would have been able to carry on a conversation, considering she was taking this stranger to her home with the intention of making love with her. It was almost midnight, the streets were quiet. They sped along MoPac, heading to Northwest Austin.

In no time, they pulled into her driveway, and they paused as the garage door opened to let them inside. Standing in the garage, the overhead light glaring, their eyes met across the car. Jo refused to think. If she did, she would send Kelly away immediately. But right here, now, she knew that was not what she wanted. Not tonight. Tonight, she wanted to lay in this woman's arms and enjoy the feelings that she brought to her. No matter that this was something Johanna Marshall did not do. Had never done. But the promise in those dark eyes was too much for her to deny. It had been too long.

They stood there for a long time, long enough for the light to blink off. Only then did they move. Kelly walked around the car to her, took her hand, and Jo led them to the door. They entered the kitchen, Jo shut the door after them and, feeling amazed at her boldness, led Kelly into her bedroom.

They did not speak aloud. Yet the energy between them spoke volumes. Jo turned and moved into Kelly's arms. Their lips eagerly sought each other, and it was clear their desire had not dimmed during the drive. If anything, the anticipation had increased it. Now, there was no audience to witness their passion, no reason for them to stop. Jo let her hands travel over Kelly's back, caressing her just as their tongues caressed each other.

She drew in a sharp breath as Kelly pulled Jo's blouse out of her jeans and began unbuttoning it slowly. She stood still, eyes on Kelly's, hands resting lightly on her shoulders. Strong hands went to Jo's bare breasts, moving over them slowly, thumbs rubbing the taut nipples.

Their breath came quickly, and Kelly drew her close, kissing her softly, then more eagerly. She pulled back as Jo tugged Kelly's shirt out. Jo wanted to touch her. Her hands trembled as she undid each button slowly. She reached behind Kelly, unclasped her bra, and then touched her breasts for the first time. They filled her hands, and she stood with her eyes closed, fingers lightly touching Kelly's nipples, feeling their hardness. Oh, they felt so good to her touch.

Kelly cupped Jo's face with her hands and drew Jo up, kissing her, her tongue tracing Jo's lips, slipping inside and over her teeth. With sudden urgency, she pushed Kelly's shirt off her shoulders and let it fall to the floor along with her bra. She let her own shirt fall behind her, and they stood together, bare breasts touching as their mouths eagerly sought each other.

Kelly's hands went to Jo's jeans at the same instant that Jo went for hers, and they both laughed softly. But the laughter died quickly, replaced with an urgency that would not be denied. Soon, they were naked, standing by the bed, both with uncertain smiles on their faces.

"Are you sure about this?" Kelly asked softly.

"No, but yes, yes," Jo replied, trying hard to ignore the fact that she was giving herself to a perfect stranger.

"You're so beautiful," Kelly whispered.

"So are you."

Jo reached for her. Their bodies touched, and then their lips sparked. Jo felt the heat assail her again thinking her legs would buckle. She knew how ready she was for Kelly, how wet she had become. Pulling the covers back, she laid down on the bed. Kelly came to her, pressing her weight on top of her, lips moving over her face and neck, her tongue snaking into her ear as Jo sighed and held her close. Kelly's fingers moved over her breasts. Jo desperately wanted her mouth there, and she felt Kelly slide down, her lips moving tantalizingly over her, tongue tracing Jo's nipple, swirling over the taut peak before covering it with her mouth. Jo groaned deep in her throat, holding her near, her hands on either side of her face. Kelly moved to the other breast, sucking it into her mouth. Jo pressed her closer, holding her there, thinking that she had never before felt such pleasure.

Kelly moved lower, her lips tracing a path over Jo's flat stomach and into the hollows of her hips, causing Jo to rise up to meet her. She whimpered softly as Kelly moved her legs apart with her shoulder. Kelly's tongue washed across her inner thighs over and over.

"Please," she begged softly, and Kelly's mouth settled over her, causing her to cry out. Her hands clutched the sheets, head arching back as Kelly's tongue moved over her, inside her, stroking her expertly as Jo writhed beneath her mouth. Dear God, she felt like she would surely explode. Closing her eyes tightly, her hips pressed up to Kelly's face. She breathed deeply, then held her breath as this woman, this stranger, brought her so close to ecstasy. She started to take a deep breath and then gasped. Suddenly, her hips stilled, pressed up into Kelly's expert mouth, as her orgasm clutched her, consumed her. She cried out loudly, shocked by its intensity.

Jo brought Kelly up to her, holding her close as her breathing calmed. She swallowed hard, eyes still tightly closed. Kelly said nothing, just let herself be held as Jo moved her hands gently over her smooth back. Before long, Jo's lips began exploring Kelly's neck. She rolled Kelly over, laying by her side, one leg pinning her to the bed.

They gazed at each other, their eyes missing nothing. Jo softly kissed her lips, tasting herself on them, and it stirred her so. Her tongue moved inside Kelly's mouth, over her lips, wetting her face. Jo kissed her neck where her pulse throbbed, her teeth nipping at Kelly's skin, sighing against it. She wanted to please this woman, this stranger whom she just met. She wanted her to feel the same intensity she felt. Her hands cupped Kelly's full breasts. She moved her mouth over them, thrilling in the feel of their softness. Kelly's nipples were hard. Jo's tongue teased them, making them swell even more before she took each of them into her mouth.

Kelly's hands ran through Jo's hair, holding Jo's mouth to her, hips pressing up against Jo's leg. Jo could feel Kelly's wetness on her leg as her hand moved down between their bodies, seeking Kelly's warmth, feeling her surge up to meet her fingers as Jo delved into her smooth, silky softness.

Jo's lips left her breast, her mouth followed the path of her fingers, kissing the warm flesh of Kelly's stomach. Her chin grazed Kelly's soft, fine hairs, and she heard Kelly moan softly, and she smiled, wanting to please her. Her tongue wet a trail along one thigh, down her leg, and up the other thigh, and Kelly begged her to touch her.

"Please. Now," she demanded.

Jo pressed her mouth to her, letting her tongue slowly move over Kelly, tasting her. She settled between Kelly's legs, hands pushing them apart, tongue and mouth quickly stroking her. She felt Kelly press up into her. When she slipped her tongue inside her, Kelly clutched at her shoulders. Her mouth sucked and her tongue swirled over her. Kelly screamed out, hips thrusting forward against Jo's mouth as her orgasm exploded.

"Dear God," Kelly breathed as her body slowly calmed.

She then laid back against the bed, arms and legs limp against the covers.

Kelly drew Jo up into her arms, one hand caressing Jo's hair. Kelly's fingers slid over her body gently before cupping her intimately. Jo pressed against her hand, wanting to feel Kelly's fingers on her, inside her. Kelly teased her, and Jo reached for her hand, placing it firmly between her legs. Kelly moved over her softness, feeling her readiness. Several fingers slowly slipped inside her and Jo surged up to meet them. Kelly moved with her, her thumb rubbing, her fingers plunging deep, as Jo's hips rose and fell with her rhythm. Her breath came quickly, and she clutched at Kelly's shoulders as orgasm claimed her. Holding Kelly inside her, she squeezed her thighs tight around Kelly's hand.

When Johanna finally relaxed, allowing Kelly to move away from her, she reached for her and held her close, hands brushing the hair from Kelly's face. She should be tired but she didn't want the night to end. Lovemaking had never been like this before. She kissed Kelly's mouth softly, gently, trying to tell her without words how she felt. Kelly lay still, seeming to understand.

They made love again and again, finally falling asleep as the first rays of dawn brightened the eastern sky.

Chapter Three

Johanna woke slowly, feeling disoriented. Her mind cleared, and her eyes snapped open. She turned her head quickly, looking at the bed. Empty.

"Oh, God," she said out loud and shut her eyes. Her limbs felt heavy, and she stretched, every muscle screaming out its protest. "What have I done?"

She rolled over and looked at the clock. Ten already. Kelly had a game at nine.

Kelly.

Johanna squeezed her eyes shut against the memories of last night, covering her face with her hands. Had she really spent the entire night making love to Kelly Sambino? Yes, she admitted, groaning aloud.

"Oh, God," she said again. She turned her head into the other pillow and took a deep breath, smelling Kelly's perfume mixed with the sweet smell of their lovemaking. "Oh, God."

Rolling back onto her side, she clutched her knees to her stomach. "What have I done?" she whispered. "Oh, God."

She lay there with her eyes closed, trying to deny the truth, but the reality of last night came crashing down around her. She hadn't had a lot of lovers, had certainly never spent an entire night making love. Even when her relationship with Nancy was brand new, she could not recall spending more than a few hours in bed. None of her experiences had ever been as consuming as this. Even now, disgusted with herself as she was, she felt a warm feeling wash over her as she remembered all the things Kelly's hands and lips had done to her.

"Oh, God," she said again. "Was I out of my mind?"

Lying still, she let her mind go blank, soon drifting back to sleep. An hour later she woke to the phone ringing but ignored it. Let the answering machine get it, she thought. She sat up, feeling light-headed, and blamed the rum. Hell, she blamed the whole night on the rum. Or, better yet, the summer heat. She rubbed her forehead and then her eyes. She stood up, naked, and looked at her clothes lying in a heap beside the bed. "Oh, God," she repeated, shaking her head.

The phone rang again, and she walked into the living room, listening as the answering machine picked up. Her grandfather's voice startled her into action.

"I'm here," she said, quickly switching off the machine and picking up the phone.

"You're late," he said.

"Oh, Harry. I'm sorry. I overslept." They had had a standing date for Sunday brunch for years. She rubbed her forehead lightly, trying to ease her headache and her conscience.

"It's okay. I can put everything on hold, Jo-Jo."

"No, no, Harry, I'm sorry," she said again. "I'll be there in half an hour."

She rushed through her shower, refusing to dwell on the night before, pulled on shorts, a T-shirt and her Teva sandals, and hurried out. Her grandfather lived on Lake Travis in a house he and her grandmother had built long before the lake had become popular with Austinites wanting to escape the city. Now, the mansions that had sprung up around him dwarfed his small, modest house.

She drove down the familiar winding drive to the house she had called home since she was twelve. After her mother, Sarah, was killed, her grandparents had taken her in and tried to repair the damage caused by the loss of her only parent. Johanna had never known her father. He had left when her mother was seven months pregnant with her and was never heard from again, but they managed to survive. Her mother worked two jobs and went to college at night, finally finishing when Jo was seven. Sarah became a teacher at a suburban elementary school, and they moved into their first house a year later, leaving the dingy apartment behind. Then, on a rainy afternoon in March, when Johanna was twelve, her mother's car skidded around a curve, colliding with a tree. She had been killed instantly.

Harry and Beth Marshall had willingly taken Jo in and saw it as their life's work to try to make her happy. Sarah had been their only child. Johanna was their only grandchild. As a teenager, she had rebelled, of course. She was a hellion, silently bitter about her loss. But that, too, passed. After high school, she enrolled at the University of Texas, graduated in three years, and then continued until she had her master's degree. She had been teaching at Austin City College for ten years now, and didn't have any desire to move on.

Harry was waiting for her on the porch, sitting in his usual rocker. She parked in the shade of the old oak tree, walked up and hugged him.

"I'm so sorry," she began.

"Nonsense," he said, dismissing her apology. "You're entitled to oversleep now and again."

Harry Marshall, eighty years old, didn't look a day over sixty-five. He had thick white hair, which he wore much too long for a man his age. But he looked fit. He still swam the lake every day, even in winter. Only his eyes showed the years, and the sadness that had been there since his wife, Beth, died.

Jo had been coming to brunch on Sundays ever since college, and because her grandmother had passed away two years before, she often stayed the whole afternoon with Harry, fishing in the lake, going on a boat ride, or just talking.

She smiled and knew he noticed the dark circles under her eyes. Four hours sleep was not nearly enough for her, especially after a night like she had spent. She lowered her eyes, hoping he wouldn't ask. He didn't.

He served them chicken over a bed of rice, fresh vegetables from his small garden and iced tea in the same glasses she remembered from her childhood. The table was crammed into a nook at the back of the house, facing the lake, and they watched the boats on the water, some pulling skiers behind them, others just cruising by. She was quiet and knew she was not being very good company. Turning away from the lake, she smiled at him, murmuring how good lunch was.

"Have a late night?" he finally asked.

"I went to a softball tournament yesterday and out to dinner," she answered, avoiding his eyes.

"Oh."

"With Betsy," she volunteered.

"You haven't brought her around in a while," he said.

"I haven't seen her in a while, either."

"Well, now that summer is here, you should have more time for your friends."

She looked up quickly. "Yes."

"I worry about you, you know."

"I know," she said. "Thank you. I love you for it."

"You need someone other than me."

He gave her a smile and said what he always said. "I wish you had someone, Jo-Jo."

"Oh, Harry, I'm fine. You know that."

"But still, I won't be around forever."

She dismissed that comment. He had been saying that since the day her grandmother had died.

After they cleaned up the dishes, they took the boat out and cruised around the lake, taking their time as they marveled over the expensive houses dotting the shoreline.

"Hard to believe we were one of the first ones out here," he said, like he usually did.

She nodded, like she always did, and smiled at him. He was all she had left, and it saddened her. He had withdrawn some since Beth had died and she knew it was a struggle for him to hang on. Part of him had died with her, despite how much Johanna needed him. He had lost his wife, his partner and Johanna couldn't even begin to know what that must be like. The devastation she had felt when Nancy left couldn't even begin to compare to the death of a spouse after fifty-two years of marriage.

"Let's go out for dinner this week," she suggested, as they were tying the boat up.

"Sure. Mexican food?"

The memory of last night flashed by, and she shook her head. "How about Italian?"

"Okay."

"Wednesday?"

"Sure."

They brought out the worn deck of cards and the pitcher of iced tea and settled at the picnic table. The breeze off the lake and the shade of a giant oak made the heat bearable. They played cards and chatted, Jo thankful for anything to keep her mind occupied. If she concentrated really, really hard, she could almost forget that she had spent last night in the arms of a complete stranger. Occasionally, though, images would sneak through and she would feel herself go hot as she saw a flash of herself on the bed, arms reaching for Kelly, silently begging for her touch.

She grabbed her glass of tea, embarrassed by her thoughts. Touching her face with the cold glass, she sighed.

"Hot?"

Jo nearly sputtered at his innocent question and pretended interest in her cards. "I'm a little warm," she said. "But I guess it's that time of year."

"I don't even think about it anymore," Harry said. "If I get hot, I just strip down and take a dip."

"Harry! You're not still skinny-dipping during the day, are you?"

Last summer, Harry's new neighbor had been near the property line, cleaning brush, and had spotted Harry in the buff, and called the sheriff's department.

"I think she sits on her porch with binoculars," Harry said, his eyes twinkling with amusement. "Maybe she's just looking for a thrill."

"They warned you that they would fine you next time, Harry," Jo reminded him.

"Oh, bullshit," he laughed. "Wouldn't that make good news? Slapping a fine on a shriveled-up old man for indecent exposure."

Then he laughed again. "But I guess that would be an indecent sight."

Jo laughed, too. Harry had not been in such good spirits in a very long time and, despite her headache, she stayed for another round of cards.

It was after three when she finally left. During the drive home she tried in vain to forget about last night. Without Harry to distract her, images of Kelly Sambino kept intruding. Her stomach did a slow roll as she remembered how her mouth had reluctantly left Kelly's breast, only to travel down her body to a warmer, wetter place.

"Oh God," she murmured.

She turned the air vent to her face, then the fan on high, stubbornly refusing to let her mind replay any more of the events of last night. Instead, she spent the rest of the drive chastising herself for acting like a wanton harlot!

She knew she was being foolish, but she parked in the driveway, not wanting to go into the garage and remember the long moments they had stood there, staring at each other across the car. But she sat in the car and remembered anyway, hands gripping the steering wheel, unaware of her accelerated breathing. She was aware, however, of the warm sensation between her legs, and her eyes closed slowly as she saw first Kelly's hands, then her mouth move over her body. She shuddered at the memory of her own urgent hands guiding Kelly to the ache between her thighs.

The low moan in her throat startled her, and her eyes

flew open. She buried her face in her hands, trying to erase the images, trying to curb her arousal.

When she went inside, her answering machine was blinking. Ignoring it, instead she took a beer from the refrigerator and poured it into a frosty glass from the freezer. Despite the heat, she went out onto the deck and sat in the shade, drinking her cold beer and staring out toward Bull Creek as the clear water rushed over the limestone bottom. She loved her house. It was a little bit of the Hill Country nestled in the foothills of West Austin. Thick groves of cedar and oak lined the creek and gave her privacy from her neighbors. It was a small creek, barely four feet deep during the wet season and only twenty-five feet across in some places, but it was a haven to her. On hot, sunny days, she would take a tube and float downstream, then paddle back up and do it all over again. The cold, spring water was a blessing during the hot days of summer.

She watched a cardinal land on her empty bird feeder and frowned. She had forgotten to buy birdseed again. The ringing of the phone echoed in the house and she shut her eyes, not wanting to talk to anyone. She knew it was Betsy, wanting to know all about last night, and she wasn't ready to talk about it. She might never want to talk about it. After three rings, the machine picked up. She let her mind go blank as she focused on the rushing water and the hungry cardinal pecking at her empty bird feeder.

Her beer finished, Jo went back inside and stood before the answering machine. She had intended to ignore it, but the flashing light beckoned her and she pushed the "play" button, her heart hammering in her chest. She expected to hear Kelly's voice, and she wasn't at all sure she wanted to.

She needn't have worried. None of the messages were from her. Betsy had called four times, and Susan Gruber, her dean from the college, had called, inviting her to a barbecue the next weekend. She didn't know if she was glad Kelly hadn't called or disappointed that she hadn't bothered. Perhaps Kelly was used to these one-night stands. Maybe she was feeling none of the anguish Jo felt.

Walking into her bedroom, she saw her clothes, still lying on the floor from the night before. She stopped, raising her eyes to the ceiling.

"Oh, God."

She gathered the clothing quickly and shoved it all into the hamper. Out of sight, out of mind, she thought.

The phone rang again, and this time she picked it up.

"Jo? Where have you been?" Betsy demanded.

"At Harry's."

"I've been calling since early this morning," she retorted.

"Yeah, well I went early this morning," Jo lied.

"You didn't make the games," Betsy accused.

"I don't remember telling you that I was going today," she said dryly.

"Well, I just assumed. . . after last night."

Johanna let that pass and rolled her eyes to the heavens.

"How did they do?" she finally asked.

"They lost the first one, then won the next two and made it to the finals but lost five to four."

"Oh."

She wanted to ask how Kelly had done but bit her tongue. She shouldn't even care.

"Listen, we're going out to Adam's Ribs for barbecue this evening. Why don't you come along?"

"Oh, I don't know," she said. "It's too hot to stand in line."

She was scared to death of seeing Kelly again, although she wondered if she had already left for San Antonio.

"Come on, it'll be fun. Bring some beer. You know they don't sell any." When Jo didn't respond, she added, "We'll stand in the shade."

Johanna finally agreed, against her better judgment. She chastised the part of her that wanted to see Kelly again, and prayed that she had already left town.

Chapter Four

Adam's Ribs was crowded, even for a Sunday. Located some twenty miles south of Austin, it had the reputation for the best barbecue around. People waited outside under the cedars, milling around the coolers of beer they had brought, waiting for tables to empty inside. Hummingbird feeders hung from every tree, and ruby-throated hummers buzzed around, dodging people as they fought for a turn.

Johanna sat in the back seat of Betsy's car while they parked along the road; the parking lot was full. They had dumped their beer into one cooler, and Janis carried it into the crowd as they looked for familiar faces. Jo had not asked if Kelly was going to be there, and they had not offered the information. She scanned the crowd, looking for their friends, spotted Kay and waved, then followed Betsy and Janis.

"Hey, you came," Kay said. "You missed some good ball today."

"I heard. Sorry you lost."

"We made it further than we thought we would. It was fun," she said.

Jo scanned the crowd, seeing Deb, Sharon, Mattie and a few others she knew. Her eyes stopped when she spotted Kelly talking to a very attractive blonde.

She looked away quickly, pretending interest as Kay, Betsy and the others talked about the last game.

"Man, Kelly came that close to scoring," Kay said, holding two fingers millimeters apart.

"Who's the girl with her?" Deb asked. Jo listened intently, ignoring Betsy's glance her way.

"I guess it's her girlfriend. She showed up for the first game and has been here all day."

Jo felt a sinking feeling in her stomach and busied herself with the cooler, digging a beer out from beneath the ice. Girlfriend? Girlfriend? Good God, she had a girlfriend? Why did this surprise Johanna? Of course a woman like Kelly *would* have one, wouldn't she? Oh, God! She had taken a stranger home from the bar, home to her house, and had made love with her all night long, and she had a girlfriend! Oh, God! She rubbed her forehead and squeezed her eyes closed tightly. What have I done? I'm no better than Nancy, she thought. She took a long swallow of beer, trying to still her pounding heart, trying to ease her shaky stomach.

Christy came over, and Jo smiled absently at her as she downed the rest of her beer. She wasn't driving. She could drink, she thought, as she reached into the cooler for another. Anything to quell the embarrassment she felt. Oh, God, what had she been thinking?

"Who's that with Kelly?" Betsy asked.

"Sherry. One of her girlfriends," Christy informed them.

One of them? Oh, God. Jo took a deep breath and smiled, pretending to be unaffected by their conversation.

"I think she's pretty much got her pick," Christy added. "She goes out a lot. I always see her with someone new," Christy continued, oblivious to Jo's discomfort.

"I would guess so," Betsy said. "She's gorgeous."

They don't know the half of it, Jo thought. Thankfully, the conversation turned away from Kelly. Jo actually was amazed with herself. She managed to contribute some, all the while keeping her eyes firmly away from Kelly and her girlfriend, Sherry. She decided at that moment that remaining celibate the rest of her life wasn't such a bad idea.

The line moved and they did also, shoving their coolers along with them. The sun was setting in the west, the air had cooled, and Jo was on her third beer. I should be at home, she thought, anywhere but here, where she had to shield her eyes from the sight of Kelly listening so intently to Sherry. Try as she might, she couldn't avoid looking at her. Kelly's head was bent toward Sherry, and she spoke to her softly, a smile on her face. Sherry was blonde and beautiful, her hair flowing nearly to her shoulders, and she frequently touched Kelly's arm when talking. Why she had to touch her, Jo didn't know. And her hair? Surely that wasn't natural.

Jo watched them, remembering last night and all she had shared with Kelly Sambino. She watched her lips and she watched her hands, thinking of them touching her intimately. Oh, what a fool she had been! She hoped she had learned her lesson, taking a stranger home from the bar, how dare she!

She looked back at Kelly and was startled to find her staring intently. Kelly turned and said something to Sherry, then made her way through the crowd toward her, her eyes never leaving Jo's. Jo wanted to turn away, but Kelly's held her captive and she waited for her.

"How are you?" Kelly asked quietly, moving between Johanna and the others.

"I'm fine," Jo managed to say.

"I'm sorry I left like that, but I didn't want to wake you," she said softly, her dark brown eyes peering into Jo's. "Well, I did want to wake you," she teased, "but then I would have been late for the game."

Jo didn't answer but she couldn't look away from those eyes.

"I called a cab," Kelly offered.

Jo shrugged and finally turned away. God, how she remembered every detail of the night before, the intimacy they had shared washing over her. She clenched her jaw, then raised her eyes to Kelly. She wanted desperately to forget everything about last night.

"Are you okay with everything?" Kelly asked.

"No," she said honestly.

"No? Jo, last night was . . ."

"Last night was a mistake," Johanna said, almost angrily, meeting Kelly's eyes. "A big mistake. I'm going to pretend last night never happened."

"Why? It was incredible."

"No," Jo said, shaking her head. She motioned toward Sherry. "Shouldn't you be getting back?"

Kelly followed her eyes to Sherry, then looked back at Jo. "Jo, she's just a friend."

"Right. So I've heard."

"I can explain," Kelly said.

"No, there's no need, really." She looked away, then back at Kelly, drowning in her dark eyes despite her best attempt not to. "Last night was something I don't care to repeat. I don't know about you, but I've never done anything like that before and good God, you've got a girlfriend! How could you?" she hissed. "Why didn't you tell me?"

"It's not like that," Kelly protested. "We're not involved."

Jo raised one hand and shook her head. "It doesn't really matter. It's none of my business."

Kelly looked frustrated. "Look, we had a relationship at one time, yes. But that's over. Jo, we're just friends. I swear. Let's go somewhere and talk, please." She tried taking Jo's hand but Jo pulled away.

"I've nothing to say to you, and I told you, it's none of my business" she whispered, just seconds before Sherry joined them.

"Kelly? Are you coming? I think we're next," she said sweetly, and Jo bit her lip. The woman looked like she had just stepped out of the pages of a magazine. Jo hated her.

"Yeah. I'll be there in a second." Kelly turned to Johanna again. "We need to talk," she said quietly. "You have to let me explain."

"Don't bother. Just leave," Jo said and turned away.

Chapter Five

When Deb called on Wednesday to invite Jo out to dinner, she still hadn't recovered from the weekend and had no desire to go out. Instead, she invited Deb to her house on Friday for steaks. It would give them a chance to catch up, maybe renew their friendship.

She had just put in a CD when Deb knocked. Jo took time to straighten the magazines by the sofa before greeting her.

"It's so good to see you." Jo stepped back from the door and motioned her inside.

Deb, holding a bottle of wine, gave her a quick one-armed hug. "You, too."

She looked around Jo's living room and nodded. "I've always loved your house. I've missed coming here."

Yes. Jo remembered, before Nancy, that Deb would sometimes spend the entire weekend with her. They would cook a meal together or just spend a lazy afternoon on the deck talking.

"I know. It's just. . . you never seemed to hit it off with Nancy."

Deb nodded in agreement. "I never liked her much, you're right. I didn't think she was right for you."

Jo forced a smile to her face and took the wine from Deb. "Well, that ended up being true." She turned toward the kitchen. "But I'd rather not talk about Nancy," she called over her shoulder. "Go out to the deck. I'll bring the wine."

Jo leaned against the counter and rubbed the bridge of her nose, trying to ward off a fast-approaching headache. She had no desire to talk about Nancy, but was afraid Deb would bring up Kelly. She certainly did not want to face questions about her.

Pushing off the counter, she grabbed two glasses, determined to enjoy Deb's company. They had been close at one time and Jo could use a friend that was single, too. She sometimes felt like a third wheel when she hung out with Betsy and Janis, although not because of anything they said or did. But still, it would be nice to have a single friend to go out with occasionally.

"Your backyard has grown up," Deb observed.

Jo handed her a glass of wine and sat down, leaning her elbows on the patio table. "I know. I've got to stop planting things. Pretty soon, I won't be able to see Bull Creek."

"Oh, no. I like it. It gives you more privacy. But if I recall, you never had much of a green thumb," Deb laughed, pointing at her potted plants, which were in dire need of water.

"I know. It's all I can do to keep the ones in the house alive. I'm always amazed when things out here survive," she said, motioning to her yard. The lot had been wooded when she bought it. Over the years she had added native shrubs and plants to give her more privacy from her neighbors. She was most proud of the stone walkway she and Harry had built years ago. She followed the path with her eyes as it twisted down to Bull Creek.

"Do you still swim?"

Jo smiled. "Well, I float in the inner tube. It's kinda hard to swim in only four feet of water."

"I guess you still go out to Harry's?"

"Every Sunday for sure. But I don't teach in the summer anymore, so I go a couple of times a week. I've been getting him to pull me in the boat."

"Well, if you wouldn't mind company some Sunday, I'd love to go skiing again."

"Sure," Jo agreed, although she doubted she would invite Deb on a Sunday. Sundays had become a ritual for her and Harry. She didn't want to spoil it by bringing an outsider.

They sat in silence, watching the antics of a squirrel as it tried to invade the bird feeder. For once, she had remembered to fill it.

Jo was aware of the uncomfortable lag in their conversation, but she couldn't determine the cause of it. They hadn't been around each other in years and perhaps it had been wishful thinking on her part to believe they could just fall into old habits. People change and she supposed they had, too.

"I'll get more wine," Deb offered, intruding on her thoughts.

Jo watched the blue jays dive at the squirrel. She wished she hadn't invited Deb to the house. Maybe they should have gone out to eat. They would have had more distractions, something other than a squirrel to stimulate the conversation.

"Are you dating anyone, Jo?"

Surprised, Jo glanced at Deb, silently watching as she refilled her glass. "No. Not since Nancy left," she said. And it was true. Her one night. . . affair. . . with Kelly could hardly have been called a date.

"I thought so, but when we never saw you around, I assumed you were seeing someone."

"No."

"I was a little worried about you the other night," Deb commented.

"The other night?"

"At the bar. You left with that. . . with Kelly Sambino."

Jo felt herself blushing. "I just gave her a ride to her hotel," she lied.

"Well, you should be thankful she didn't try anything. I hear she's quite the stud in San Antonio."

"Stud?"

"You know what I mean. Lots of parties, lots of different women hanging on her arm. Christy said she dates several at one time, keeping them all in the dark about the others."

"Really?" Jo wondered why Deb felt the need to tell her all this. Frankly, she could not care less about Kelly Sambino!

"Yeah. I didn't really like her that much," Deb said.

"I thought she got on fine with the team." Jo was surprised that she felt the need to defend Kelly.

"Oh, she can play ball, all right. But, you know, her attitude was so... California. She was just so conceited."

Jo held her tongue. If there was one thing she had learned about Kelly, it was that she was not the least bit conceited. But Jo said nothing, forcing what she hoped was a smile onto her face.

"And you know that woman that showed up for the Sunday game?" Deb continued. "That wasn't even her current girlfriend, according to Christy. Sambino had been dating someone from their softball team."

Jo rubbed her eyes quickly, wishing Deb would lose interest in this subject and go on to something else. She did not want to discuss Kelly with Deb or hear all these things about her. It was what she had suspected, of course, but it only made her. . . *affair.* . . with Kelly that much worse. She pinched the bridge of her nose again, her headache having settled behind her eyes.

"I really can't stand women like that," Deb continued.

"Well, I really don't know her," Jo said. "And I doubt I'll ever see her again."

"Count yourself lucky that she didn't try anything," Deb repeated. "She apparently has something women like, although I just can't see it."

Are you blind? Jo thought. Deb's remarks didn't fool her. Deb was simply jealous and Jo wondered why this had not occurred to her earlier. Deb had been single most of the time Jo had known her. She was shorter than Jo, a little heavier, too, but Jo thought she was cute. Not drop-dead gorgeous like... well, like some women, but she was still cute. Jo remembered that Deb had rarely dated, though. Deb would never stir the kind of passion that Kelly apparently invoked in... some women.

"Well, she didn't try anything. Maybe I just don't have what she likes." Jo gave a nervous laugh. It would be a miracle if she made it through the evening.

Chapter Six

June turned into July, and Johanna cursed the heat as she sat on her black inner tube in Bull Creek. It was nearly four o'clock The temperature, which had topped out at 102, had now dropped to a sultry 99. Paddling into the shade, she splashed cold water on her shoulders, now tanned a golden brown from her weeks in the sun. She was spending many afternoons with Harry, fishing the lake and cooking fresh catfish and bass for their dinners. She had even joined Betsy and Janis for dinner on a couple of occasions, though she refused to discuss that sordid weekend in June. Betsy had asked only once, and Johanna had lied and said that nothing had happened. Betsy left it at that, even though they both knew she was lying. She had not accepted Deb's second invitation to dinner. The first had been too stressful and she was afraid Deb would bring up Kelly's name again. Kelly had called her only once and thankfully, the answering machine was the only one who heard the whole message. Once she heard Kelly's voice, Jo had deleted the message without even listening to it.

Now, with July coming to an end and August just around the corner, Jo was thinking ahead to the upcoming semester. Soon she would be busy planning her classes, attending faculty meetings, and living her life as scheduled.

She didn't allow herself to think about Kelly Sambino, even during the lonely, hot nights of summer, when she swore she could still smell Kelly in her bedroom. The trick was staying busy. She went to Hippie Hollow, the only nude section of Lake Travis, and swam naked in the clear waters. She made a trip every morning to Zilker Park and swam laps in the cold, cold waters of Barton Springs. In addition to their afternoons and Sunday brunches, she had dinner once a week with Harry and sometimes he drove the boat while she skied. She stayed busy. She didn't think about Kelly Sambino. She didn't think about the wonderful night they had shared, making love until dawn.

"Right," she said aloud. Who was she kidding? Did a day go by that she didn't remember Kelly's kisses? Laying her head back on the tube, she closed her eyes to the sun, remembering every detail of that night. She felt herself go warm all over again and knew it had nothing to do with the July heat. She tipped herself out of the tube and submerged in Bull Creek, laying on the limestone bottom as the cold water rushed over her, cooling her senses.

Soon, the neighbor's dog started barking, welcoming them home, and she cursed her lack of solitude. The kids would be splashing in the water soon. Oh, she was getting cranky, she thought. Thirty-six and already a grouchy old woman!

Later, one evening in early August, Susan, the dean of the English department and a good friend, called her.

"Arnie wants to do steaks on Saturday. Come over. Plus, I want you to meet someone. We've hired a novelist for the semester to teach the creative writing class."

"That's great," she enthused. "Of course I'll come."

Jo knew that the department had wanted to get a published author for this class. Last semester, they had to settle for a graduate student, as the university had snatched their lone candidate from beneath their noses.

She was somewhat relieved at Susan's call. It meant that the fall semester would soon be starting, and she could get on with her familiar, routine life and leave the awful confusion of the summer behind her.

On Saturday, she ironed her shorts while standing in the spare bedroom wearing nothing but her underwear. It was hot and humid outside, and she had the air conditioning turned down to 70. She wasn't sure how many more weeks she could take of the heat. Laughing to herself, she wondered how many years now had she been saying this same thing?

She tucked a white T-shirt in her shorts, slipped on her sandals and drove to Susan and Arnie's house, only ten minutes away. They had been friends for years and when Susan was appointed dean four years ago, it had done nothing to alter their friendship. She treated Jo as an equal, at college and away. Jo frequently joined them for dinner during the school year.

She pulled into their drive, parking beside a Ford Explorer, which she assumed belong to the novelist they had hired. She wondered what he would be like. Austin City

College wasn't small, but it couldn't compare to the University of Texas, where most of the teaching talent went.

She rang the doorbell, then let herself in. She heard the faint sound of voices in the front hall. Making her way through the familiar living room to the sliding door, she stopped abruptly when she saw Kelly.

"Oh, God," she whispered. "No, no! It can't be."

The woman she thought she would never see again, the woman she had hoped she would never see again, the woman she couldn't stop thinking about, was but a few feet away.

Kelly Sambino stood beside Susan, a beer held casually in her hand as she listened intently to Susan's story. Johanna's eyes traveled up her long, tan legs, slim waist, past her full breasts, to her face, and the memory of their night together came crashing through like a wave racing to shore, hitting her full force, as if it had only been yesterday that they had been so intimate with each other.

"Oh, God," she said again, suddenly feeling a little sick.

Arnie was sticking a match to the charcoal and, as flames erupted, he stepped back. Jo stood in the living room, indecisive. She had half a mind to flee, and if Susan hadn't looked her way at that moment, she might have done just that.

"Jo, you're here. Come on out," she beckoned. Johanna bravely walked the few feet to the door, and despite her better judgment, slid it open.

"Hi," she said, looking first to Arnie, then Susan, then finally resting her eyes on the very dark ones of Kelly Sambino. Oh, God, she thought, I can't do this.

"I want you to meet Kelly Sambino. We're lucky to have her," she said, and Jo walked towards them.

"Hello," Kelly said and stuck out her hand.

"Hello," she answered and took that hand, her heart pounding in her chest.

"Stole her from St. Peter's in San Antonio," Susan said.

"Really?" Jo was surprised by the steadiness of her own voice.

Kelly released her hand slowly, and Jo quickly shoved hers in her pockets, trembling.

"Oh, yes. She's going to be a great addition to our staff," Susan went on, and Jo couldn't drag her eyes away. What is happening here?

"Get yourself a beer, honey," Susan told her.

"Yes, I think I better," Jo muttered, ignoring the amused look Kelly gave her.

"How're you doing, Arnie?" she asked, as she walked to the large, red cooler and dug a beer out from beneath the ice.

"Great. You?"

Jo paused for a moment, then lied. "I'm doing good."

Arnie moved closer to her and asked in a low voice, "So, what do you think of the novelist?"

"I think we're lucky to have her," Jo said, repeating Susan's words.

"Yeah," he agreed, and they both looked at Kelly Sambino as she listened to Susan, who was rambling on as usual. Arnie had once said that Susan could talk to a tree and Jo knew this to be true.

She stood directly under the ceiling fan, feeling the breeze hit her face. It wasn't cool by any stretch of the imagination but still, it was a breeze. Arnie had converted the covered patio into a garden and nearly every available space had been filled with potted plants and flowers. Jo had always envied Arnie his green thumb.

"How do you keep these things alive in this heat?" she demanded.

He laughed. "Watering helps, Jo. I doubt the five plants on your deck have seen much of it."

"I'm down to three, and I watered them at least two weeks ago."

"Well, if I didn't think you'd kill them. . . I've got some cuttings just getting started." Then he gave her shoulder a friendly squeeze. "Maybe I'll put something together for you."

How he found the time, Jo didn't know. He worked at one of the busiest accounting firms in Austin. During tax season, Susan rarely saw him.

Jo watched him walk away, shaking her head at his version of casual dress; starched shirt and slacks. But then, he was the stereotypical accountant. Short, pleasantly round, and balding. And he never left the house without a tie!

She glanced to where Susan and Kelly still stood. Their contrast was striking. Kelly was tall, young, fit. Susan was short, entrenched in middle age, her dislike of exercise evident. Kelly was even darker than Jo remembered. Susan rarely went out into the sun unprotected and her pallor appeared almost unhealthy compared to Kelly's tan. Susan's blonde curls seemed to glow next to Kelly's dark hair.

Jo noted that Kelly's hair was longer than she remembered but then again, so was her own. Her eyes took in other details: the small, gold chain around Kelly's neck, the diamond earrings, the lone ring on her right hand, the slender, gold watch on her left wrist. Jo stared at Kelly's hands for a long moment, remembering all that those hands had done to her, then made herself look away, flushed. She tipped her beer and took a long swallow, again thankful for the ceiling fan. The light breeze cooled her hot cheeks. Oh, God, how can this be happening? Why me? She brought her eyes back to the woman standing across from her and met an impudent smile. Damn her!

Susan brought Kelly over to Johanna and smiled, too. "You two get acquainted. I've got to start the salad." She left them, and Jo stood quietly, refusing to meet Kelly's eyes.

"So, how have you been?" Kelly began.

Johanna turned on her quickly. "What the hell are you doing here?" she asked quietly.

"I'm going to teach the creative writing class." She lowered her voice. "You're lucky to have me," she said, grinning.

Jo nearly let a smile slip out, then remembered her anger in time. "Why here? At my school?" she demanded, looking over her shoulder at Arnie.

"Hey, don't flatter yourself. I don't make it a habit to change careers based on one-night stands." She gave Jo a mocking smile. "Especially ones that are such big mistakes."

"How would I know? You probably pick women up at the bar all the time," Jo hissed.

"As do you," she shot back.

"How dare you? I told you, I have never done anything like that before."

"And you want me to believe you?"

"It's the truth," she whispered. It was very important to Johanna that Kelly know how out of character that night was for her. She wanted Kelly to take all the blame, she realized.

"How do you know it's not the truth when I say the same thing?" Kelly asked.

"You're the one with the reputation, not me. You're the one who's involved . . ."

"Sherry and I are not involved!" Kelly insisted.

Jo met her eyes head on and did not flinch. "Listen, I don't want to talk about it."

"Fine."

"Good."

"Okay then."

"What? Do you have to get the last word in?" Jo asked.

"Yes!"

Damn her!

But Kelly smiled. "You know, when you get all riled up like this, you're kinda cute and your accent is really pronounced."

Jo bristled. "I don't have an accent."

"Sure you do."

"I do not."

"A Texas drawl," Kelly continued. Then she raised her eyebrows teasingly. "I think it's very sexy."

Kelly turned away before Jo could protest, and Jo silently fumed at her retreating back.

During dinner, Arnie asked Kelly where she grew up, and Jo found herself listening with interest, though she refused to look up.

"California. San Francisco."

"Really? How long have you in been in Texas?"

"Just two years this summer," she said, not seeming to mind the questions.

"What kind of name is Sambino?" he asked.

"Arnie, you are full of questions tonight," Susan said, apologizing to Kelly.

"It's okay. Sambino is Italian."

"That's where you get your dark looks, then," he said.

"That's about all. My family is not very traditional. No one speaks the language and certainly, no one can cook Italian," she said with a smile.

"Why not?" Susan asked.

"Oh, my father remembers a little, I guess, but it mostly died with my grandfather," she said, and Jo looked up then, curious. "My grandfather's family lived in New York, most of them barely spoke any English. He moved to California right out of high school and married the very non-Italian, very blonde daughter of his boss. His family refused to accept his marriage and basically disowned him."

They were all quiet, waiting for her to continue, and Jo thought she was not going to, but then Kelly looked up and smiled. "That was in the early thirties. By the time their letters had crossed, with explanations from him and pleadings from them, she was pregnant with Aunt Isabel and the matter was settled. So, they stayed in California and he just lost his roots, I guess."

"So do you still have family in New York?" Jo asked, surprising herself with the question. She was not at all interested in Kelly Sambino, she reassured herself.

"Oh, I imagine so. You know the reputation that Italian families have," Kelly laughed. "I've never had any contact with them, and I've certainly not met any of them. No one in my family ever has."

"That's sad," Jo said. She, on the other hand, had no one else in the world except her grandfather. Well, she supposed her father was somewhere, but she didn't even know his name.

"I guess. But that's the way they wanted it. My immediate family is close. My father has three older sisters and they all have four or five kids. I have a younger brother and an older sister and my parents are great. We have a very happy family."

"Both of your grandparents are gone?" Jo asked.

"Yes. My grandfather died two years ago at the age of 88. He was a wonderful man," she said, and Jo felt a lump rise in her throat. She saw Kelly in a different light and was touched by the gentleness with which she spoke of her large family. Jo envied her.

"You'll be going back to California someday, I guess," Arnie said.

"I suppose. All of my family is still there and I don't really have any attachments here. I like Texas, don't get me wrong. But I'm not used to your summers and I don't think I'll ever be."

Jo couldn't help but laugh. She had been here her whole life and she wasn't used to them yet either!

"I know you graduated from Stanford," Susan stated. "And you were in the University of California system for a time. You obviously love teaching. But now you want to be a novelist?"

Kelly laughed. "Yes. And I know only a handful of writers actually make a living at it. But I really love to teach, too. I doubt I'll ever get away from it completely."

After dinner, Susan made coffee, but both Kelly and Jo declined. It was just too hot. Instead they both accepted a glass of wine and everyone went back outside to the patio. The evening was pleasant, and they chatted quictly, listening to the crickets and cicadas in the yard. Johanna wondered why Kelly hadn't mentioned to Susan and Arnie that they knew one another, though she was glad she hadn't. She would just as soon forget the whole thing anyway!

As they were leaving, Kelly opened the door to her Explorer and waited, looking at Jo across the hood of her car, a teasing smile on her face.

"That wasn't too bad, was it?" Kelly asked.

"Yes. It was a terrible surprise."

"Oh, now, come on, you enjoyed yourself, admit it."

"The meal was pleasant," Jo conceded.

Kelly shrugged and got in her Explorer, slamming the door. Jo stood and waited until Kelly's window buzzed down.

"What are you doing here, really?" Jo asked again.

"I was tired of San Antonio and when this position was brought to my attention, I took it." Kelly smiled mockingly at her. "I didn't even remember that you taught here."

Their eyes held for a long moment, then Jo looked away.

"I really don't want that night brought up again. Please," she said quietly. "It's bad enough I have to live with it without everyone else here knowing."

"Yeah, well, you should have thought about that before you seduced some stranger in a bar with those gorgeous blue eyes of yours," Kelly shot back.

"I did no such thing!" Jo protested.

"No? Then who was that woman making such beautiful love to me that night until the early morning hours?" Kelly asked softly. "Until we were too sated for even one more kiss?"

Jo stared at her, speechless, her pulse pounding in her head.

"Hey, but don't worry. I have no desire to broadcast what an easy catch I was that night," Kelly smiled mischievously. "I do have a reputation to maintain, after all." She pulled away and waved out the open window, leaving a stunned Jo staring after her.

"See you around," she called, as she sped down the street.

"Oh, God," Jo fumed. "That woman infuriates me!"

Chapter Seven

Jo had her usual Sunday brunch with Harry, then spent two other mornings with him, fishing. Once the semester started, she would have little time to visit, other than on weekends.

"How are you doing, Jo-Jo?" he asked suddenly, when they were cleaning the catfish they caught for dinner.

"I'm fine. Why do you ask?"

"You've just seemed unusually quiet, that's all."

She knew she had been preoccupied because she was worried. She hadn't been able to get Kelly Sambino out of her mind all week, and was dreading running into her at the college. It was going to be a long semester.

"I guess I'm just thinking about work," she said. It wasn't all a lie.

Betsy called later that week, and Jo shoved a bookmark into her novel.

"You'll never believe who we ran into at the ball field," Betsy said.

"Who?"

"Kelly Sambino."

"Now, why doesn't that surprise me?" Jo muttered under her breath.

"What?"

"Nothing. So, did you talk to her?"

"Of course. She sat with us the whole game. Why didn't you tell us she'd taken a position at Austin City College?"

"I guess because I haven't talked to you. I just found out on Saturday myself."

"Well, it's great, isn't it? She's going to play third for us when the fall season starts."

"Yeah. Great," Jo said, thinking she wouldn't be making any more games this year.

"Why don't you sound thrilled about all of this?" Betsy asked sarcastically.

"Why should I?"

"I thought you said that nothing happened between you two."

"So? Does that mean I have to want to work with her?" she snapped.

"Hey, sorry," Betsy muttered. "Who put a bee up your butt?" She hung up.

Jo replaced the phone, rubbing her forehead. She knew Betsy was not really angry. They had too much history between them for that.

She had first met Betsy Gannon in the girls' locker room in high school. The new kid with the curly red hair had been hurrying past Jo's locker when she slipped and landed on her rear, practically at Jo's feet. Betsy had laughed along with everyone else, reached for Jo's outstretched hand and pulled herself up.

"Very graceful," Jo remembered telling her. "I see the years of dance lessons have paid off."

"Oh, great, a smart ass."

They had become friends after that and had remained friends when Betsy had first confessed her attraction to another girl. Then, years later, when Jo was in college and struggling with her own attractions, Betsy had been there for her. Just like she had been there for Jo when Nancy had left. And Janis, too. They had been together so long, it was hard for Jo to picture a time when Betsy had been without Janis.

They had remained the best of friends throughout the years, and Jo had never hesitated confiding in them. But this thing with Kelly . . . Jo wasn't ready to share it, even with Betsy.

The next week, two days before the first faculty meeting, Johanna went to her office, like she did each year. She prided herself on being organized, and she planned to take notes and begin her first two lectures.

Her office was immaculate: every book in its place, every paper put away. She could not work with chaos or disruptions. The freshman English classes she taught were really boring to her, after ten years, but the composition and rhetoric classes were more enjoyable. She loved to read, and she spent the morning going over her lists of books, deciding which ones her classes were going to review this semester.

A door opening and then slamming shut down the hall startled her. Soon, footsteps and then whistling followed. She frowned, annoyed. The other faculty members were usually more quiet than that.

A door opened again, just down the hall, then quiet, finally. She listened, then went back to her notes. Her head shot up at the sound of loud music blasting just a few offices away. The Rolling Stones? She closed her eyes.

"Who the hell is listening to the Stones?" she muttered, massaging her eyebrows and the bridge of her nose.

Johanna walked to her door, sticking her head outside briefly before slamming her own door shut. She sat back down, the music somewhat stifled. Turning to her computer, she tried to shut out the noise and concentrate. A short time later, a knock interrupted her. She scowled.

"Come in," she muttered.

Kelly Sambino stuck her head in.

"I should have known," Jo said under her breath.

"Hey, I didn't know anybody else was here." Kelly leaned against the door, tan legs stretching out beneath her shorts. "What are you doing?"

"I was trying to work." It had been nearly two weeks since she had seen Kelly, and Jo's hungry eyes took her in.

"Oh. Am I disturbing you?"

"Yes. How can you possibly work with all that racket?"

"I work better with something for background noise."

"Well, I work better in absolute quiet!" Jo exclaimed.

"And you want me to turn it down?" Kelly asked, the ever-present mocking smile firmly in place.

"I want you to turn it off," Jo said pointedly.

"Now, Jo, you need to learn to compromise." Kelly turned to go. "I'll turn it down a notch."

"Or three!" Jo called after her.

Kelly turned back and frowned at her. "What can you possibly be working on? Susan said you've been teaching here for ten years. You'd think you'd have it all down by now."

"Do you think I teach the same thing now as I did ten years ago?" Jo asked defensively.

"Has English changed?"

Jo ignored her and turned back to her computer. "I also teach a composition class."

"Oh, I hated that class," Kelly groaned.

"Well, now that you're a writer, I bet you're glad you had to take it," Jo shot back.

"No, not really." Kelly shook her head. "I loved creative writing, though."

"They're practically the same thing."

"Far from it."

Jo glared at her with piercing eyes, and Kelly walked out, the mocking smile unchanged.

"Infuriating woman," she muttered, noting the door again standing open. Jo rubbed her forehead, trying to ward off a headache.

Her phone rang suddenly, and Johanna stared at it as if it were a foreign object. After the third ring, she heard Kelly yell from down the hall.

"Pick up the damn phone!"

Jo did and held it to her ear, not missing the amused chuckle on the other end.

"Do you want to go out to lunch later?" Kelly asked.

"No!"

"Okay. Your loss." She hung up, and Jo held the receiver to her ear a little longer, then put it back. The woman was going to drive her insane!

At ten minutes to twelve, Jo heard the radio shut off and a door close. Whistling began in the hall, then stopped.

"See ya later," Kelly called loudly and continued whistling.

"Thank God. Maybe now I can get some work done."

But she found she couldn't. The quiet mocked her, and

after a few more minutes she left her lecture unfinished and snapped off the computer. It was going to be a very long semester indeed.

She picked up Chinese food that evening and drove to Harry's, stopping on the way for a bottle of wine. He greeted her with his usual hug, but she thought he looked tired.

"Hi. Are you okay?" she asked gently.

"Yeah. Just missing my Beth today."

"I'm sorry, Harry," she said and held him close.

"Two years, you'd think I'd be used to it by now," he sighed.

"We'll never be used to it, I guess." She kissed his cheek. "I love you."

"I love you, too, Jo-Jo." He pulled away, wiping a tear from his cheek. "That smells good," he said with forced cheerfulness.

She peered at him searchingly. "You're not planning on leaving me, are you?" she demanded.

"No, honey. Not just yet," he said quietly. Then he gave her a crooked grin. "I've got to find you someone first."

"I'm fine."

"I just want you to have someone to take care of you."

"I don't need anyone, Harry," she insisted, busying herself with dinner.

"We all need someone, Jo-Jo." He carried their plates to the table as she brought the wine. "Don't let that fool Nancy turn you off love."

"You never liked her, did you?"

"I liked her because you did. Now, I don't have to like her anymore."

"Well, Harry, don't worry. I'm fine. I'm happy."

"Are you, honey?"

She met his eyes and forced a smile. "Yes," she said quietly.

That night, as she lay in bed, waiting for sleep to come, she realized that she was far from happy. Something was missing in her life. She had her career, but that suddenly wasn't enough. Maybe it was her age catching up to her. Or Harry's. He wouldn't be around forever, she thought sadly. And then who would she have? No one. Just her friends, who she rarely saw as it was. And most of them had partners. Why was it so difficult for her to find someone? Before Nancy, there had not been anyone special, and they had dated for years before Jo had finally allowed her to move in. Look where that had gotten her!

She felt very old suddenly. It seemed like forever since her huge crush on the basketball player, her first kiss from the cute little blonde in her chemistry class, her night with Jill Stanton, the first woman she had fallen in love with.

Her thoughts went to Kelly Sambino, and she tried to push them away, but Kelly's image remained. She didn't even like the woman. But that wasn't entirely true. There seemed to be two sides to Kelly. One, teasing and infuriating. The other, intense and passionate. Jo had seen them both. Kelly was refreshing, she realized. She smiled a lot and seemed happy. It was one of the things that had drawn Jo to her. She remembered that first time she had seen her, laughing and talking with the opposing team, with her own teammates. Then that night, much later, when they were alone and intimate, there was no teasing about her. She was serious and passionate. They had spoken little during the night. Actually, Jo remembered, they hadn't spoken at all. At least not with words.

She rolled over, staring at the clock as it ticked to midnight. She didn't want to remember her night with Kelly Sambino. She closed her eyes and thought of Adam's Ribs, of Kelly talking to Sherry, of Christy reminding them that Kelly had lots of girlfriends, that Kelly went out a lot. She thought of Deb's words at dinner that night, how Kelly had a reputation of dating several women at once. Jo certainly didn't need that in her life again. Nancy had had a reputation as a runaround and Jo had gotten involved with her anyway. She had been seduced, and then abandoned. Four years down the drain. Another three feeling sorry for herself. Where had the time gone?

Chapter Eight

The first faculty meeting took place the week before registration, and Johanna was nervous. She had not seen or spoken to Kelly since that day in her office. Betsy had not said anything about their softball games, and Jo had not asked.

Now, as she walked in and took a seat, she looked for her. Her eyes scanned the room, seeing familiar faces, smiling at those who were her friends. She spotted Kelly across the room, talking to a couple of coaches, listening intently as they spoke. Her easy smile appeared often, and she launched into conversation, her hands moving, and Jo imagined her talking about softball or some other sport.

People took to her, she realized. She was easygoing and friendly and not at all hard on the eyes! Kelly brushed her hair out of her face and caught Jo staring at her although Jo tried to look away quickly. Damn her!

The president opened the meeting, as he always did, commenting favorably about the last year and urging them toward another successful semester. He announced the recent retirements, then introduced the newest members of the faculty, and Jo watched as Kelly stood up when her name was mentioned. She was wearing shorts and a T-shirt and didn't seem in the least out of place among the dresses and suits surrounding her. It figures, Jo thought, as she squirmed in her pantyhose and tried to spread her toes in her too-tight shoes.

After endless speeches, they broke for lunch, and Susan grabbed her on her way to her office.

"Let's walk to Ralph's," she suggested.

"I've got work to do," Jo insisted.

"Nonsense. Classes are two weeks away and knowing you, you've already got your first month planned."

Jo couldn't help but laugh. It was true. She was boring and predictable. "Okay. A quick lunch," she agreed.

"Great. I've asked Kelly Sambino, too. You know, she doesn't know a lot of people in Austin yet."

Right, Jo thought. Just the entire softball team and probably half the gay women in town by now!

Kelly was waiting for them at the back door, and she greeted Jo with a genuine smile, then quickly replaced it with the mocking one that Jo had come to recognize. Jo ignored both of them.

During lunch, Jo learned that Kelly was staying in an apartment not far from where Jo lived and that the softball team was undefeated so far. Jo pretended not to be interested, but she took in every word. Each time those dark eyes flashed her way, she looked away quickly, feigning interest in the other tables around her. Kelly wasn't fooled.

That afternoon, as Jo was making notes on her computer, Kelly stuck her head in.

"What are you doing?" she asked.

"Working," Jo said, without looking up.

"Again?"

"Always."

"I'm going to Hippie Hollow. Want to go?"

"No way," she said quickly. The last thing she wanted was to be swimming naked with Kelly in the lake. Lord, no!

Kelly shrugged. "Suit yourself." She left without a goodbye and Jo listened to her footsteps fade down the hall.

But a swim did sound good. She picked up the phone, called Harry and invited herself over for dinner.

They swam together in the lake, then took the boat out, and before she knew it, Jo was cruising by Hippie Hollow, wishing she had her binoculars. She searched for Kelly among the rocks, then felt foolish and sped away, smiling at her grandfather. He always laughed at her, saying that when she was out there swimming, she didn't like boats cruising by her looking for a cheap thrill!

They ate on the deck in the twilight, watching the sun turn the water a rosy orange.

Chapter Nine

The first day of classes were madness, as always. Half of her students did not yet have their books and as she went over the syllabus, she saw several of them frown and check their schedules, making sure they were in the right class. The routine was comforting to her. Every year it was the same and every year she gave an assignment the first day, eliciting groans from the students. She was not an easy teacher, never had been and she was proud of it.

At twelve-thirty, Kelly stuck her head in Jo's office.

"Have you had lunch?" she asked.

"Yes," Jo lied, eyeing the unopened bag of chips on her desk.

"Okay. Just thought I'd ask." Kelly shrugged and walked away. Jo wondered how her first day had gone and wished she had asked her.

Every day that week, at exactly twelve-thirty, Kelly walked in and asked Jo to lunch. Each day, Jo declined.

"You do eat, right?" Kelly finally asked on Friday.

Jo smiled at her. "Yes." She put her pen down, pushing away the papers she had been grading.

"How's your first week been?" she asked.

Kelly seemed surprised at her question. "It's been great. Terrific, actually. I've got some talented kids. Very inquisitive."

"Good."

They stared at each other in silence, then Kelly gave her a mocking smile. "I'm going out for Italian. Sure you don't want some?"

"No."

"Don't like Italian?" Kelly asked with a raised eyebrow.

"I love it," she said.

"Really?" Kelly asked softly, teasing.

"We are talking about food, right?"

"Of course," she said and left.

Jo stared after her, smiling.

When Jo returned to her office at three, there was a small box on her desk with a note. "Leftover lasagna. You must be starving for some Italian by now."

She grinned and blushed and quickly turned around, expecting to find dark eyes mocking her from the doorway. There were none.

She ate the lasagna while she graded her papers, refusing to think of the woman who had left it.

Jo was the last one to leave, as it was Labor Day

weekend, and she was probably the only one without plans. She spent the entire weekend with Harry at the lake, and he was thrilled to have her sleeping over. He made a huge breakfast on Saturday and they took their time over it, watching the lake crowd with boats and skiers. On Sunday, they got up before dawn and went down to the pier to fish. Two unlucky bass volunteered to be their brunch, and they were back at the house while the morning was still cool. They drank coffee on the deck, listening to the lake come alive.

The next week, Kelly again stopped to ask her to lunch, and Jo always refused, but she had begun looking forward to the asking. If twelve-thirty came and went, she found she couldn't work until she heard footsteps outside her door, and she quickly picked up a pen and pretended to work. She had half a mind to accept one day, but each day she refused. It would do her no good to be alone with Kelly Sambino.

The following Friday, Kelly stopped by. She didn't ask her to lunch. She asked Jo to dinner.

"No. I've got plans," Jo said. It was true. Susan and Arnie had asked her over for steaks.

"Oh. Someone special?"

"Yes, as a matter fact," Jo said. It wasn't a lie.

Kelly stared at her for a long moment, and Jo met her gaze.

"Who?" Kelly asked.

"That's none of your damn business," Jo said quickly. Let her think what she wanted.

“Hot date?”

“Perhaps.” Jo was aware that her voice was shaky.

"Well, lucky you," Kelly said. "I guess I'll see you next week, then."

Jo nodded, and Kelly left, whistling down the hall.

Her last class was over at three, and she hurried home.

She wanted to relax in the creek before the neighbors got home, and she quickly donned a swimsuit and took her beer down to the water.

Settling in her tube, toes skimming the cool water, she floated along lazily. The current in early September flowed at a snail's pace. It would soon be too cold for her to get in, but the temperature still climbed into the 90s these days. Another few weeks and the first cold front would blow in, bringing a promise of autumn and more comfortable weather.

She wore jeans to Susan's and immediately wished she had worn shorts. She tugged at the blouse around her neck, feeling the sweat trickle under the collar. Turning into their drive, she slammed on her brakes and stared in disbelief at Kelly's Explorer. Damn her!

Several seconds passed as she sat with the engine running, overwhelmed by indecision. She could always leave and call them with some excuse, but Susan would never forgive her. She got out and slammed the door, resigning herself to face the consequences. It was her own fault. She was the one who had implied to Kelly that she had a date tonight. Damn it all!

She rang the doorbell and went inside. They were on the patio, and she could see the three of them sitting in lawn chairs, the charcoal already glowing. Susan waved to her through the glass, and Jo forced a smile, refusing to meet the amused eyes of Kelly Sambino.

"Jo, how are you?" Arnie asked, already handing her a beer.

"Good, Arnie. Thanks," she said, taking the bottle from him.

"Hi," Kelly said, good-naturedly, and Jo gave her a quick smile, not meeting her eyes.

"Hello."

"Jo, Kelly tells me that you two have yet to do anything

together. I'm surprised. You're both single and near the same age. Why haven't you taken Kelly out and shown her the town? You know, she doesn't know many people in Austin yet."

Jo stared at Susan in silence. Was this her way of telling Jo that she knew Kelly was a lesbian, too? No. Susan was clueless. Just as she had been about Jo. She then slowly slid her eyes to Kelly.

"I thought you knew quite a few people here, what with softball and all."

"No, not really. No one special." Kelly had an amused glint in her eye.

Jo cursed under her breath. Damn her lies! Would she ever learn?

"I see. Well, I'm not sure that we would have the same interests," she said vaguely.

Susan seemed perplexed at the conversation and looked from one to the other.

"Maybe not," Kelly said. "Do you like softball?"

"Oh, sure she does. She has friends that play in the city league," Susan offered, and Jo glared at her.

"Really? Who? Maybe I know them," Kelly said innocently.

"I doubt it." Jo drained her beer. Why did this woman cause her to drink so?

Kelly smiled, and Jo got up to take another beer from the cooler. How did she get herself into these messes?

Susan went inside to get a dip and some chips while Arnie left them to check the charcoal. Jo looked out into the yard, ignoring the woman sitting next to her.

"Are you enjoying yourself?" Kelly asked.

"Immensely," Jo said dryly.

"Yes, it is a special evening," she grinned.

Jo ignored her.

"I'm sorry if I spoiled your night," Kelly said softly.

Jo looked at her, surprised by her sincerity.

"I shouldn't tease you so."

"No, you shouldn't," Jo agreed.

Kelly leaned forward suddenly and met Jo's eyes.

"Do you think about that night?" she demanded.

Jo drew in a sharp breath but didn't look away. She slowly shook her head, afraid to answer.

"Why are you lying?"

"If I think about that night, it's not in a pleasurable way," she admitted.

"No? It was very pleasurable, the way I remember it," Kelly said softly. “I can still taste your lips, your skin. I can still remember what you felt like when I. . . . ”

“Stop. Please,” Jo begged.

Jo clenched her jaw and forced herself to look away from those deep brown eyes. Arnie’s return saved her from replying, and Kelly sat back in her chair, her eyes still resting on Jo.

After dinner, they went out to the patio, each with a glass of wine. Jo was hoping that Kelly would leave first, so she wouldn't have to walk out with her, alone, but she didn't. They chatted about the first few weeks of school, and Jo wondered if Arnie ever got tired of all the college talk. She listened with interest as Kelly discussed her students and her style of teaching, so different from Jo's. Jo realized how boring she must be compared to Kelly. They had several of the same students, and she wondered if they compared the two teachers.

Finally, it was time to leave and they walked out together, saying good-bye to Susan and Arnie inside. Jo walked immediately to her car, but Kelly followed.

"How long are we going to keep this up?" Kelly demanded.

"I don't know what you mean," Jo said, as she unlocked her car.

"This pretending that nothing happened between us."

Jo turned on her. "I don't know what you want me to do," she said quietly. "I've tried to put it from my mind, but you show up here, throwing it in my face daily. I want to forget it, don't you see?"

"Well, I can't forget it," Kelly stated. "I don't want to forget it."

Kelly stepped closer, and Jo took a step back.

"Something happened that night, Jo."

"No."

"Yes, it did."

Jo sighed. "That night proved only one thing. I was temporarily insane."

"Why do you say that?"

"Because that wasn't me," Jo admitted. "I just don't do that. Not with someone like you." She wanted to take the words back immediately.

She saw the pain flash across Kelly's face, then she masked it, giving Jo a mocking smile. "Someone like me? Am I that bad?"

"I've been told. . . well, that you see a lot of women at the same time." Jo got angry. "And I hate the fact that I was just one more in a long line of hundreds, probably."

"Hundreds? Is that what you think?"

Jo didn't answer.

"Well, no wonder you don't want to have anything to do with me. I'm a bum, with a hell of a reputation," she added quietly.

Jo was sorry she had even brought this up. "I didn't mean..."

"Yes, you did. I'm sorry, Jo." Kelly walked away. "I'll leave you alone. Let you forget all about it. Let you plead temporary insanity."

She got in her Explorer and drove off, and Jo sat in her car for a very long time before leaving. She had hurt Kelly. All this time, she had pretended that Kelly didn't have feelings, but she did. Just as Jo did.

Chapter Ten

She didn't see Kelly at all the next week, and, much as she hated to admit it, she missed her. She found herself looking for Kelly to stick her head in the doorway at lunch, asking her to go out when they both knew Jo wouldn't. But she never came. One day, Jo saw her walking down the hall, away from her, arms loaded with books. Jo almost called to her, but at the last moment she didn't. It was better this way.

Betsy called and invited her to the softball game that week. Jo thought about going but declined. Instead, she spent another night alone, watching a meaningless movie on television and wishing she had gone to the stupid game. She couldn't keep avoiding her friends for fear of seeing Kelly.

The next week, when Betsy called, Jo accepted. She had not spoken at all to Kelly since Susan's dinner party and had only seen her the one time. She had half a mind to ask the dean if Kelly was still teaching there but knew that would only cause questions.

The September evening was cool and pleasant. Jo drove with her sunroof open, the stars twinkling overhead as she sped down MoPac, denying the anticipation she felt. It had nothing to do with seeing Kelly, she insisted.

She walked with her lawn chair to the field and squeezed in beside Betsy and Janis.

"I haven't seen you in ages," Janis complained. "Why don't we go to dinner sometime?"

"Let's do," Jo agreed. She had gotten there early for once. The players were just warming up, and she quickly located Kelly, who was tossing a ball back and forth with Kay. Kelly was smiling and chatting with Sharon, who was standing next to her, and Jo felt a tightening in her stomach. Kelly's pants clung to her thighs and Jo vividly remembered how they looked without pants on, how lean and smooth they were. She closed her eyes and looked away.

"Let's try that Mexican food place out by your house," Betsy suggested

"The Palacios Cafe? I've been there with Harry. It's very good," Jo said.

"How about one day next week?"

"Okay, sure."

The players took the field. Kelly jogged to third, oblivious to Jo sitting there. She smoothed the dirt around the bag, pounded her glove and yelled encouragement to Sharon on the mound. Jo was taken back to that early June day, that hot summer day when she saw Kelly for the first time. The attraction she felt then was nothing compared to what she felt now. Her eyes stayed glued to Kelly, following her every movement as she charged a ground ball and threw to first, long arm whipping the ball ahead of the runner.

Kelly's first time up, she lined a clean single up the middle, then raced to second as the center fielder bobbled the ball. Jo watched as Kelly's long legs carried her gracefully to the bag. She finally looked away, embarrassed. People might start to notice her staring.

"Want a beer?" Betsy asked.

"Yes, please. I forgot to bring any."

"We've got plenty," she said and handed her one, her eyes missing little.

Jo stood and cheered with the rest when Kelly hit a long fly ball over the center fielder's head that rolled all the way to the fence. Kelly jogged around third and followed Kay to the plate and it was only then that she saw Jo. She paused and their eyes met for an instant before Kelly looked away and slapped hands with her teammates. They won easily.

Of all the things that Jo had wondered about, Kelly's age was not one of them. Now, as she watched her, she tried to guess. She was very fit, which could be misleading. Was she even thirty? The question stayed with her as the spectators mingled with the players after the game. The next two teams took the field, and the fans moved their chairs out of the way, leaning them against a tree as they drank beer and talked about the game.

Kelly didn't come talk to her, and Jo was hurt. But who could blame her? Jo talked to Kay and Deb and covertly watched Kelly chatting with Betsy and Janis. She should go over, she thought, excusing herself from Kay and walking toward them. Kelly watched her, but she didn't smile, not even when Jo smiled first.

"You had a good game," she said.

"Thanks," Kelly replied as she took a beer from Betsy.

"Only one home run tonight, Sambino. You're slipping," Betsy teased.

She smiled briefly and shrugged apologetically. Sharon joined them and Betsy and Janis turned to her, leaving Kelly and Jo standing alone.

"How old are you?" Jo asked suddenly.

"What?" Kelly was surprised.

"How old are you?" she asked again.

"Why?"

"Because I don't know."

Kelly leaned forward and grinned. "Don't worry. You didn't rob the cradle."

Jo blushed and looked away. "That's not why I was asking," she said quietly.

"No? I thought you needed another reason to hate yourself."

"No. I have plenty, thank you," she said before she could stop herself. She expected Kelly to offer a quick retort, but instead, she gave Jo her usual mocking smile.

"I'm thirty-five. Old enough to know better," she said and turned away.

Jo watched her leave, carrying her bat and glove in one hand, the beer still clutched in the other.

"Why is she leaving already?" Sharon asked.

Jo just shrugged, her eyes following the lone figure to the parking lot. A car pulled alongside her, and Kelly bent down to talk to the driver through the open window. Jo watched as Kelly walked around the car and got in. As the car turned, Jo recognized Lucy, Deb's friend, and her heart clutched painfully.

Chapter Eleven

September crawled by, at least for Johanna. Her classes seemed a drudgery this semester, the usual joy in teaching was somehow missing. She found herself just going through the motions and had to mentally stop and kick herself every once in awhile. She worked late, she was organized to the point of being absurd . . . still dull and boring. Predictable. Oh, she had gone out to dinner with Betsy and Janis, and had even gone to another softball game, but she and Kelly had not spoken. Their eyes met once, when Kelly had walked to the plate to bat, but that was all. It was enough, really. Just that one look had caused Jo's heart to tighten in her chest, caused her to remember every detail of their lovemaking. The image of them lying together, naked, on her bed flashed in front of her eyes as if it had only happened yesterday.

On the last Saturday of the month, Jo was sitting on her deck, reading and sipping iced tea when the phone rang. She considered letting the machine pick up, but she hurried inside anyway.

"What are you doing?" It was Betsy.

"Reading."

"Don't you ever get tired of that?"

Predictable. Boring. Yes, she was tired of that. "It's a hobby," she offered.

"It's all you do."

"Is not."

"Yeah? Well, good. Tonight you can go out with us."

"Out? Where?"

"Lakers. The team's going out. It's Sharon's birthday. Some of them are going out to eat first, I think, but Janis and I are just going to meet them there. We'll pick you up at eight," she declared.

"No. I'm not going to the bar. I told you, I don't. . . ."

". . . like to go out during the semester," Betsy mimicked her. "I know. But can't you break your rule for once? It's a birthday party," she pleaded.

Jo thought about spending another Saturday night alone or with Harry, who was beginning to wonder about her always hanging out with him, and decided to break her own rule. It might be fun. She refused to even consider that she was going because she hoped Kelly might be there.

"Okay. But I'll take my own car."

"Great. Come by the house and you can follow us."

Johanna dressed with care that evening, though she adamantly refused to think of any particular reason why. She ironed dark slacks until they were crisp and tucked in a loose-fitting pale green blouse. She applied her makeup with care and lightly sprayed perfume, all the while avoiding meeting her own eyes in the mirror.

It was a pleasantly cool evening and that, alone, put her in a better mood. Gone, or so it seemed, were the scorching days of summer. She tapped on their door and waited patiently until Janis let her in.

"It's nice that you're going with us, Jo." Janis motioned her in, and Betsy handed her a glass of wine.

"We were just going to sit on the patio for a minute," she explained, and they sat in lawn chairs, sipped their wine, and caught up on each other's lives.

"I'm glad you decided to go," Betsy said.

"I felt like a night out," she said defensively. Jo wondered just how much they suspected about her and Kelly. She should have told them but frankly, she was too embarrassed.

"Can you believe Sharon is only thirty?" Janis asked.

Jo grinned and squeezed Janis's arm. "Speaking of birthdays, I believe yours is just around the corner," Jo teased.

"Two weeks. And Betsy is threatening to have a party," she groaned. "Like I want everyone to know I'm forty."

"Who doesn't know you're going to be forty?" Jo asked mischievously. "I think a party is a great idea."

"Nothing big, honey," Betsy assured her. "Just a handful of friends."

They got to the bar before nine, and it was not crowded. Deb was already there, as were Sharon and Mattie, sitting together and talking quietly. They had shoved two tables together and had chairs enough for twelve.

Jo grabbed Betsy's arm and whispered to her. "Are Sharon and Mattie seeing each other?"

"We think so, but they haven't said anything and we haven't asked."

"They make a cute couple."

"Happy birthday, Sharon!" they chorused, as they walked up.

"Thanks."

"Are you finally thirty?"

"Finally?"

"Yeah. Now you're officially a part of the older crowd," Betsy said.

"I'm not sure I like that," Sharon retorted with a good-natured laugh.

"Hey, you don't have a choice. The years just keep on coming," Janis said.

Jo's eyes scanned the room and the dance floor, and she didn't even pretend that she wasn't looking for Kelly. She apparently had not gotten there yet. Jo relaxed. Going to the bar, Jo bought drinks for Betsy, Janis and herself, and then sat stiffly, trying not to stare at the door.

When Deb asked her to dance, Jo hoped her surprise wasn't evident. She and Deb had never danced before.

"You haven't been to a game in awhile," Deb accused.

Jo tried to pull back from her too-tight embrace. "I've been busy at the college," Jo replied. And it was true. Mostly.

"Maybe you could spare an evening next week. We'll go see a movie or something," Deb suggested.

"Okay. Call me," Jo agreed, although she was already planning an excuse. For some reason, she did not want to go out with Deb. Their disastrous dinner date earlier in the summer had been enough to convince Jo that she and Deb had grown too far apart in the last seven years.

Deb nodded and pulled Jo close to her again. Deb danced well but Jo couldn't help but compare her to Kelly. Through no fault of her own, Deb just didn't measure up. Jo felt stifled being held so tightly. There were none of the tingly feelings that she got from Kelly's touch. Her heart beat its same, even rhythm.

"We should dance more often," Deb said.

"I don't know that we've ever danced before," Jo reminded her.

Deb pulled her closer still, and Jo found her breasts smashed against Deb's much larger ones. She had to force herself not to pull away.

"You feel good in my arms," Deb whispered softly, and Jo was certain she had misunderstood. She hoped she had misunderstood.

The song ended, thankfully, and saved Jo from answering. Deb led her back to the table, still grasping her hand until Jo politely pulled it away. Jo suddenly was overcome with a case of nervousness, a tightening in her stomach and a hammering pulse. She knew instinctively that Kelly was there, close by, and she cursed her body's reaction. Still standing, she looked around, spotting Kelly coming back from the bar with a drink. She looked beautiful, wearing tan slacks and a navy blouse. Jo found herself staring. Kelly stopped and looked up, as if she knew Jo was watching. Her eyes met Jo's from across the crowded room. They held each other's gaze for a moment, and Jo shuddered when Kelly's glance dropped to her lips briefly. Then she smiled, the genuine smile that Jo had not seen in forever. Kelly came toward the table and Jo, her knees weak, sat down, picking up her drink with trembling fingers.

It really wasn't fair, she thought again. Kelly was just another woman. A very attractive woman, to be honest, but still, it didn't warrant Jo's body turning to jelly at the mere sight of her. She's just a runaround, she reminded herself. Another Nancy. And she refused to consider, even for a second, that Kelly was any different.

They didn't speak, but each time Jo looked up, Kelly's eyes were on her. Johanna danced with Deb again, and when she got back, Kelly met her with questioning, raised eyebrows. But Jo had no interest in Deb, other than as a friend, and she hoped Deb felt the same. They had known each other too long for anything else. But still, the way Deb was dancing, the way Deb held her, all led Jo to believe that Deb had suddenly developed an attraction to her. . . and was acting on that attraction. But there could never be anything there for Jo. Deb did nothing for her libido. Unlike . . . no, she wouldn't allow herself to think about it again!

Jo knew full well she would decline if Kelly asked her to dance, but was surprised that she didn't. Not wanting to hurt her feelings by refusing, she was thankful she didn't have to. Kelly never asked, not once. Instead, she danced with nearly everyone else at the table, paying Lucy, who was sitting next to her, special attention. Jo was forced to watch them across the table as they talked and laughed quietly together, as if they were good friends. Or something else. Jo didn't want to think about *the something else*. . .

Later, when Trisha Yearwood's soft, slow ballad came on, Jo's eyes raised automatically to Kelly's. It was the same song they had danced to in June, and Kelly's eyes peered into hers for an eternity.

"Dance with me, please," Kelly pleaded softly.

Jo shook her head, no, but Kelly was already standing, reaching for her. Jo stood on shaky legs and took the hand Kelly offered, icy fingers wrapping around Kelly's warm ones. Jo moved into Kelly's arms with an ease that surprised her, and Kelly held her lightly. Jo rested her hand on Kelly's shoulder. Their eyes met as Kelly moved with her on the floor, legs brushing together as they danced. Jo pushed all her thoughts aside when Kelly pulled her close, letting out her breath slowly, trying in vain to still her racing heart.

The song ended much too quickly, and they pulled apart, their eyes lingering.

"Thank you," Kelly said, without any hint of teasing.

"You're welcome," Jo answered softly.

They sat at the table and ignored one another again, both pretending interest in the conversation taking place around them. A few songs later, Kelly again asked Johanna to dance, and she didn't even try to resist this time. It was futile, really. Her body had a mind of its own. She could not stop the desire that was building inside of her.

Jo walked into Kelly's arms. Kelly held her closer than before. Jo moved her hand along Kelly's shoulder, brushing her hair. She tipped her head back and their eyes collided. There was no teasing or amusement there, only a hint of desire that Jo was sure Kelly was trying to hide. Jo pulled her eyes away, trying to veil her own desire.

Kelly's warm hand moved lower on her back, pressing Jo closer still as their breasts touched lightly. Jo felt the heat rush through her body and knew she had lost control. They danced slowly, feet barely keeping time with the music, but Jo didn't care. Faces pressed together, Jo inhaled deeply, smelling Kelly's sweet scent, the scent she remembered, the scent of summer.

When the song ended, Kelly didn't immediately release her, and Jo held her near for countless seconds. She was on fire, and she no longer cared who was watching them. She felt Kelly's lips brush her ear, and Jo let out her breath, unaware she had been holding it.

Kelly held her hand as they walked to the table, her thumb lightly caressing Jo's palm. Even though Jo knew she should pull away, she couldn't. She had been craving these feelings Kelly stirred in her. She did not want a repeat of that June night, but she couldn't deny herself this small pleasure that Kelly gave her.

When she and Betsy went to the ladies' room, Jo refused to meet her questioning eyes.

"Are you having a good time?" Betsy asked.

"Yes," Jo said, nervously running a hand through her hair, refusing to meet her own eyes in the mirror.

They stopped at the bar and got fresh drinks, then rejoined the others. The bar was crowded, as was their table. Smoke rose, a light cloud hovering against the ceiling, talk and laughter all around them. Jo sat down and sipped her drink, her eyes following Kelly as she took Lucy out on the dance floor. Jo remembered them driving off together after the softball game. She assumed that Lucy must have been going to all the games. She was young, single and attractive. Kelly danced close with her, too. The pang of jealousy that hit Jo was so unexpected, it startled her. Lord, she certainly had no reason to be jealous. She and Kelly were nothing to each other. She certainly had no hold on Kelly. She didn't want one, for that matter. Why on earth should she be jealous? But as she watched them, the feeling was undeniable. Was Lucy experiencing the same feelings that Jo had, being held so close by Kelly? Having those warm hands caress her back? Were they dating? Jo pulled her eyes away from them and swallowed her jealousy, feeling very alone.

Later, the disc jockey's voice spoke softly over the speakers. "For all you lovers out there, let's get dark and slow." Cheers went up and the lights dimmed. "Here's three in a row for some slow dancing."

The dance floor went dark, and Betsy took Janis's hand and pulled her up.

"Let's dance, honey," she said.

Sharon and Mattie did the same, as did most of their table. Kelly didn't ask Lucy, thankfully. Lucy went to the floor with someone Jo didn't know. Jo lowered her eyes then, afraid that Deb would ask her to dance, but someone else claimed her. Jo let out her breath slowly. It wasn't Deb she wanted to dance with.

Kelly and Jo were left alone at the table. Jo looked up, her gaze finding Kelly. Kelly smiled softly, and Jo answered it.

"Come on," Kelly whispered.

"I don't know. . . " Jo hesitated.

"Come on," Kelly said again, reaching for her hand, and Jo knew it was pointless to resist.

Kelly led her to the dark floor, now very crowded, and they squeezed in among the other couples. It was too dark to see well and Jo was thankful. She didn't want to see Kelly's eyes, didn't want Kelly to see what her own might reveal. But she didn't hesitate as she moved close, into Kelly's waiting arms. Jo circled her back, holding her tightly as she felt Kelly's warm hand burning into her flesh, searing her back. They held each other, bodies caressing, legs touching, thighs brushing, hips straining to meet. Their breasts were pressed tightly together. Jo squeezed her eyes shut, willing herself not to remember what it was like to lay naked with Kelly, to make love to her, but she remembered. She remembered every detail of Kelly's body, how soft it was, how lean and strong it was, how warm it was. She remembered Kelly's lips on her, her tongue on her, and she trembled in her arms. Jo just wanted to be held and caressed like that again, to feel her touch again.

Kelly brought her left hand close to her body and danced that way, cradling Jo's hand to her chest. Jo's other hand had a life of its own, her fingers moving in Kelly's hair at her neck. They barely moved, bumped by other couples who were in much more of a hurry. They continued their slow pace around the floor, both savoring this brief, unexpected time together.

When the first song ended and faded into the second, they didn't miss a step. Kelly released Jo's hand and slid both arms around her, blending Jo into her body, both hands now caressing her back. Jo's freed hand slid slowly up Kelly's shoulder, and she touched her face, her fingers lightly tracing Kelly's cheek, thumb touching Kelly's lips. Oh, how she ached to kiss those lips.

They said nothing. Not one word. Jo knew that if they had, she would have been able to resist. She would have remembered Sherry, the beautiful blonde. She would have remembered Christy's words about Kelly's list of girlfriends. She would have remembered Deb's warnings. She would have thought of Lucy. But they didn't speak. There was no need. Their bodies spoke for them.

When Kelly turned her head, Jo was waiting, and their lips met, softly, gently, and Jo opened under her, accepting her tongue, meeting it with her own. How she wanted this woman! Kelly moved her away from the dancers, and Jo felt the wall behind her. She reached blindly for Kelly. They took what they both needed, what they both wanted, up against the same wall as before. Pent up desire, now released, stormed through them. They had been so hungry all these months, and now they could feast. Jo forgot about the others in the room. It was just the two of them, as their lips moved together eagerly.

The third song began softly, and Kelly moved her hands between them, her back shielding Jo from the other dancers, caressing Jo's breasts. Jo cried out, and Kelly's mouth was there, covering hers as her fingers traced Jo's swollen nipples through her shirt. Jo's hands, on either side of Kelly's face, held her near. Her mouth couldn't get enough of Kelly. Their kisses were hot, wet and hard. Her own hands moved down, yearning to touch Kelly. They settled on her full breasts, cupping them intimately.

"Do you remember?" Kelly demanded. "Do you remember how it felt when I touched you? When I was inside you?"

Jo groaned and pulled Kelly hard against her. Her legs

opened and Kelly pressed her thigh there, causing Jo to cry out again.

"I remember your hands on me," Kelly whispered. "I remember your mouth on me, your tongue inside me."

Jo felt drugged, and she strained to touch Kelly through her blouse as her mouth opened to Kelly's insistent tongue.

"Do you remember every detail of that night?" Kelly demanded.

"Yes, you know I do," Jo breathed into her mouth.

Disoriented and confused, Kelly moved her again onto the dance floor. She wasn't ready. She had not had nearly enough of Kelly's sweet kisses, but seconds later the song ended, and the lights were turned up. She was stunned by the desire she saw in Kelly's eyes, sure that her own revealed as much. She felt captivated by those eyes. She couldn't look away, and she was very sorry that the slow songs had ended. The other dancers left the floor, and they soon drew apart, their eyes still glued to one another.

"You know I want you," Kelly said bluntly.

"Yes."

"You want me, too," she accused.

"Yes," Jo admitted. "But I can't."

"You're a very stubborn woman."

"I'm sorry," Jo whispered.

Kelly simply nodded, and they walked back to the table, hands still clutched together. Jo was surprised a short time later when Kelly stood up and said she was leaving. Jo expected, at the very least, another dance with her. She told everyone good-bye and that she would see them at the game next week. Telling Sharon to have a wonderful birthday night, she gave Mattie an exaggerated wink. She looked at Jo for only a second and gave her a quick smile.

"See you at school." And she was gone.

All the joy had gone out of the evening for Johanna, and

she stayed only a little longer, reluctantly dancing with Deb again, feeling smothered by being held so close to her. She didn't want to wonder why Deb's touch did nothing for her, why her touch could not arouse the same feelings Kelly's had.

Driving home with the sunroof open and the window rolled down she let the cool breeze blow across her face. She drove slowly on the empty streets, not in a hurry to get to her lonely house.

That night, after her shower, she crawled naked into bed and only then did she allow herself to think of Kelly. She waited for the shame and guilt to come, but it didn't. What they had done, they had both wanted, and they had both wanted more. Yet Jo was grateful Kelly had not pressed. If she had insisted they leave and come here to her bed, Jo would have agreed without hesitation, and she would have been miserable in the morning. It was not what she needed. Kelly was not for her, despite what Jo's body said. The attraction between them was real, genuine, but that was all there was — all there ever could be. Johanna knew she would never be able to let Kelly into her heart. She had been hurt too badly before by someone just like her. She didn't want to go through that again. Ever.

Chapter Twelve

Sunday was a beautiful fall day, and she spent it with Harry. Instead of their usual brunch, they drove to Fredricksburg, had lunch at an outdoor cafe, then walked the streets of the old German town, window shopping and spying gifts for Christmas. Artists displayed their talents on the sidewalks and spectators paused to appreciate the local talent. As they walked arm-in-arm through the crowded streets, Harry reminisced about the town, how it had grown from a small berg to the touristy bed-and-breakfast town it was today.

Later that afternoon, they drove back to Austin through Johnson City, home of the late president, and stopped at the famous beer joint in Luckenbach for a cold longneck. They sat in the shade of the giant oaks and watched a washer tournament that some of the locals had started.

"Beth and I used to come here and play washers," Harry mused, a faraway look in his eyes.

Jo watched as young and old alike attempted to toss round, metal washers into cups that were buried in the sand.

"It doesn't look like a lot of fun," Jo admitted.

"Well, just a different kind of fun," he said. "Now, Beth, she had the eye. She could put that washer in the cup every time." He tapped Jo's leg and pointed. "Watch."

A man about Harry's age turned the washer nervously in his hand as he eyed the cup, nearly twenty feet away. Then, with a graceful underhanded toss, sent the washer sailing through the air. The small crowd cheered when they heard the washer land in the cup.

They took their time finishing the beer, both of them enjoying the washer game.

"Are you doing okay, Jo-Jo?" Harry asked on the way back.

"I'm fine."

"You're so quiet lately. Do you need to talk?"

"Oh, Harry." She laughed. She had always been able to tell him anything. She had cried on his shoulder many a night after Nancy had left.

"You're troubled about something, honey."

"Yes. I guess I am," she admitted.

It was his turn to laugh. "What's her name?"

"What makes you think it's because of a woman?"

"Because I've seen that look before," he said simply.

"Yes. I've met someone."

"And?"

"I like her," she admitted.

"And that's not good?"

"I don't think I want to like her." She glanced at him. "She's not my type."

"If she's not your type, why do you like her?" he asked.

Good question. Why, indeed? Because she's like Nancy? Kelly is nothing like Nancy. Except for her reputation, Jo conceded.

"I don't know." She smiled at him. "I'll be fine, Harry. Don't worry."

He reached over and patted her leg, then was silent. She loved him for it.

The next day at school, she was dreading running into Kelly. What would she say to her? But she didn't see Kelly all day.

The next day, at twelve-thirty, a light knock on her closed door startled her. Glancing at the clock, she swallowed, knowing who it was.

"Come in," she called.

Kelly opened the door and stood leaning against the frame, dressed in her familiar jeans and T-shirt. Jo lowered her eyes quickly.

"Lunch?" Kelly asked.

"Oh, no, I don't think so," Jo said, tapping away on the computer.

Kelly was silent until Jo finally stopped and looked at her.

"Are you okay?" Kelly asked quietly.

Jo nodded. "Yes, I'm fine."

"Good." She looked at her for a moment longer, then smiled mischievously. "I was going to go for Italian. You still do like Italian, don't you?"

Jo laughed and felt some of the tension slip away. "Yes. I still do," she smiled.

"Good." Kelly shoved away from the wall. "Seriously, I'm going to the sandwich shop on the corner. Want me to bring you something?"

"Actually, a tuna on wheat sounds good. Extra mustard."

"Ugh," Kelly said with a grimace and left.

The days got back to normal for them. At least, what Jo perceived to be normal. Neither of them mentioned the night at the bar, and Jo was thankful. Kelly came each day at lunch again. Jo politely refused the lunch date, but often asked her to bring her back something.

One day, Kelly waited at her door while Jo was on the phone with Harry. When she hung up, Kelly was glaring at her.

"Who's Harry?" she demanded. "Do you lead a secret life, or what?"

Jo laughed. "Harry is my grandfather."

"Grandfather? Why do you call him Harry?"

"I don't know." She shrugged. "I've always called him Harry."

Kelly surprised her by coming into her office, something she rarely did. She pulled out a chair and sat down, casually leaning one ankle across the other knee.

"I just realized how little I know about you. Tell me," she insisted.

"Tell you? Tell you what?"

"About you. About your life."

Their eyes met and held, and Jo felt her pulse race unexpectedly. "What do you want to know?" she asked.

"Parents?"

Jo shook her head. "My mother was killed when I was twelve. I never knew my father."

"So Harry raised you?"

"He and my grandmother."

"Is she still around?"

Jo shook her head. "No. Beth died two years ago."

"Anybody else?"

"No. Just Harry and me," she said quietly.

"Oh." Kelly was quiet for a moment, then leaned forward, closer to her desk. "What about your love life?" she asked.

Jo laughed, a blush creeping into her face. "What about it?"

"Do you have discarded girlfriends all over Austin?" she asked seriously.

"Of course not. I only have one ex, and she moved to New York with the woman she was cheating on me with."

"Oh." Kelly nodded.

"Oh, what?" Jo asked.

"That explains a lot," she said. "How long were you together?"

"Why are you asking me all this?"

"Because I want to know."

"Four years."

"Lived together?"

"Two."

"In your house?" she asked.

"Yes," Jo nodded.

"In the same bed you have now?"

Jo blushed again. "Yes," she said quietly.

"How long ago?"

"Three years."

"Okay," Kelly said and smiled.

"Are you quite finished?"

"Of course not, but that's enough for now." She stood up, leaning a hip against Jo's desk, and Jo stared at her, letting her eyes rest for a moment on Kelly's beautiful brown ones. She had missed looking at them.

Kelly smiled at her sweetly. "Now, what about lunch? How long are you going to keep turning me down?"

"As long as it takes."

"I won't keep asking forever," she said.

Jo laughed. "Thank goodness."

"I mean it," she said softly.

Jo met her eyes. "I'm afraid to be alone with you," she admitted.

"Please don't be. I would never force the issue." She was serious.

"And that's supposed to make me feel better?"

Kelly laughed, knowing very well what Jo was thinking. "Anyway, we won't be alone. The restaurant will be crowded with people."

"Like the dance floor?" Jo blurted out, before she could stop herself.

Kelly smiled. "No, not like the dance floor. Not unless you want to dance around the tables."

Jo laughed. "Okay. I'll have lunch with you. But I have a class at two."

Kelly smiled, and Jo noticed how her eyes sparkled. "I'll have you back at one forty-five," she promised.

Chapter Thirteen

They did not go out to lunch the next week, but Jo did ask Kelly to bring her a sandwich on a couple of occasions. Johanna had wanted to go, but she thought better of it. Kelly had started coming into her room to visit and during their talks Jo learned more about her, especially about her college days at Stanford.

"So you were a big college jock?" Jo asked around a mouthful of sandwich.

Kelly nodded. "That's where all my troubles began."

"Troubles?"

"Women."

"So many women, so little time?" Jo teased.

"Something like that." She met Jo's eyes without flinching. "I wasn't a very nice person back then," she said sadly. "I dated . . . a lot."

"Hundreds?"

Kelly grinned. "I wasn't that good. But it was just so easy for me. It was like there were groupies following the team around."

Jo nodded. "I remember. I had a crush on the basketball team. Lindsey Morgan, in particular. I made every game, home and away."

"I can't picture you chasing after the basketball team."

"Well, I didn't really chase," Jo admitted. "And I didn't actually ever sleep with any of them. I just had a huge crush. I wouldn't have known what to do, anyway. I was still a virgin," she confessed without blushing.

"I slept with the gym teacher when I was seventeen," Kelly volunteered, and Jo nearly spit out her sandwich.

"You're joking?"

"It's not something I'm proud of," Kelly said. "Of course, in college, it made for a great story."

Jo leaned back, trying to absorb this.

"I've shocked you," Kelly stated.

"I don't know why I'm surprised."

"That was a long time ago, Jo. I suppose we've all done things when we were younger that we'd like to take back."

"I don't know if you could call twenty-eight young, but I wish I had never gone out with Nancy Stewart," Jo said.

"Was your relationship really so bad that you wish it hadn't happened? Surely there were some good times," Kelly suggested.

"I'm sure there were," Jo said. "However, her cheating, and then leaving, have pretty much clouded my memory."

They ate in silence while Jo studied Kelly. There was so much she wanted to ask Kelly, but she was afraid her questions might be perceived as interest on her part. Which it was, of course, but Kelly didn't need to know that.

"Have you ever been in a long-term relationship?" Jo asked, her curiosity finally getting the best of her.

"Just once." Kelly lowered her eyes and her voice softened. "That's really why I left San Francisco."

"What happened?"

"It's ironic, really. I had just started working on the book and I was hardly ever at home."

"You were teaching then?"

"Yes. I could work uninterrupted in my office and that's where I stayed until late most nights." She put her sandwich down and folded her arms on the desk. "Kathy thought I was seeing someone. Instead of confronting me, she decided to have her own affair." Kelly paused, and Jo didn't miss the pain in her eyes. "With one of our good friends."

Jo sat quietly, waiting for Kelly to continue.

"I hadn't been out with any of our friends in months. I'd been so involved with my book I hadn't even realized it. Anyway, she had already convinced them that I was cheating on her. I had very little sympathy." She tried to smile. "It was a pretty big mess."

"Why did she just assume you were cheating on her?"

"It was my fault," Kelly admitted. "I got so involved with the book, I just let everything else in my life go. Not just Kathy. My students, too. I was seldom prepared for my classes."

"That's hardly license for someone to go and have an affair."

"Well, as you so frequently bring up, I had a reputation to contend with. And it was easier for her to think I was seeing someone else. I mean, how do you compete with a computer?"

"So, you've always dated? A lot?"

Kelly's eyebrows shot up. "You mean, have I always had this nasty reputation?"

"Well, you go out a lot," Jo said. "Or you did in San Antonio."

"How do you know?" Kelly demanded.

"Or so I was told," Jo corrected.

Kelly nodded. "I went out a lot, yes. How else are you going to meet people? That doesn't mean I slept with them all." Kelly looked pointedly at Jo. "Do you sleep with everyone you date?"

"I don't date."

Their eyes met and held.

"Never?" Kelly asked.

Jo shook her head. "Not since Nancy."

"Don't you get lonely?"

Jo shook her head again. "I have a small circle of great friends. I have Harry. I'm perfectly happy," she said, knowing she was trying to convince herself as much as Kelly.

"Then that night this summer. . . ."

"I don't really want to talk about that," Jo said.

She was saved by the phone, and as she talked with one of her students, Kelly cleaned up their lunch, gave her a silent wave good-bye, and left.

On Friday, as they were eating hamburgers and sharing french fries, Jo asked about Kelly's novel. She thought it was a much safer subject than their dating habits.

"Sheer luck, really. I mean, I think it's good, but there are a lot of books out there that are really, really good. But we'll see. If it's a success, then I'll quit teaching and concentrate on writing full time. If not, I can still teach and write in my spare time."

"Are you writing now?" Jo asked.

"No, not really. I've got some notes and ideas for another one, but I haven't really started yet. I want to see how this one fares."

"Well, I'm impressed. I hope it does well," Jo said sincerely.

"Thanks. It'll be out soon, so I'll force you to read it."

"Did you write when you were in college? I mean, school newspaper, that sort of thing?"

"Oh, no. Only the nerds did that! I was into sports."

They both reached for a french fry at the same time, and Jo grabbed one of Kelly's fingers instead.

"Hungry?" Kelly teased.

"Sorry," Jo murmured.

"Why don't we go out for dinner tonight and talk?" Kelly asked suddenly.

"No, thank you." Jo sipped her drink, refusing to meet Kelly's eyes.

"Why not?" Kelly asked.

"Because I don't want to spend time with you, that's why." Jo put her burger down and looked at her.

"Why not?" she asked again.

"Because I don't want to like you any more than I already do," she confessed.

"Why don't you want to like me?"

Jo frowned at her. "Because it's no good, that's why."

"You're wrong. It was very good, Jo."

"That's not what I mean. This is not just about sex, about this attraction between us," she said quietly. Her door was still open and she hoped no one was outside in the hall. She wrapped up the rest of her uneaten burger and tossed it in the trash.

"Are you attracted to me?" Kelly asked, eyebrows raised.

Jo didn't answer.

"Can't you even say it to me?"

"I don't want to get involved with you," she admitted.

"We're already involved," Kelly said. She threw the rest of her burger out, too.

"No, we're not."

"Yes, we are, whether you like it or not."

"Oh, Kelly, please. We're going in circles here." Jo stood up and walked to the door. "I don't want to have this conversation with you."

Kelly watched her for a moment in silence, then walked to the door, too. "Okay, fair enough. I understand. You're attracted to me but you don't like me. Or you don't like what you think you know about me, is that it?"

Jo saw that Kelly was hurt, but said nothing.

"In case you haven't noticed, I'm attracted to you, too. I want us to get to know one another, to see if there's something here. Jo, this summer. . . ."

"No. Kelly, don't turn that into something that it's not. I had too much to drink, I was. . . ."

"Temporarily insane. Yes, I know."

Kelly raised her hands in defeat. "I'll leave you alone, Jo. I'm sorry I've been bothering you, but I guess you're right. There's nothing between us after all." She turned and walked away without looking back.

Jo hated this. She wanted things to remain the same. She liked Kelly's teasing, her asking her out to lunch, but she didn't want their relationship to progress. She didn't want to be alone with her. Not because she feared Kelly but because she feared herself. She had no defenses where Kelly was concerned. It would be too easy with Kelly. But she just couldn't allow herself to take a chance. Kelly was not for her. And the sooner they both realized it, the better.

Chapter Fourteen

Kelly's invited?" Jo demanded. "I thought you said just a few friends."

"Will you get over it already?"

"I don't know what you're talking about," Jo murmured, while setting the table.

"Fine. Pretend you don't," Betsy told her, standing with her hands on her hips and a very disconcerting look on her face. "Kerry and Shea are coming. Kay is bringing that cute girl she had with her at the bar, Toni. Remember her?"

"She looked so young."

"Yeah. She's just out of college, I think."

"Deb?"

"No. We're not really that close with Deb. Anyway, if we invited her, where would it stop? We'd just have the whole softball team out here."

"But Kelly Sambino?" Jo asked again.

"We like her, Jo."

"She suggested the meal tonight," Janis added, when she stuck her head out of the kitchen.

"It's your birthday. Why are you cooking?" Jo asked her.

"It's lasagna. Betsy wouldn't know where to start."

"You know very well I can't cook," Betsy reminded Jo. She took the forks out of her hand and pushed her toward the kitchen. "You're making me nervous. Go pour the wine or something."

"I just wish you'd told me she was going to be here."

"Jo, she's not going to bother you. I told her to bring a date," Betsy said.

"A date?"

"Yes. You could have brought someone too, you know."

Jo glared at her for a second, then went in search of the wine. Great! Not only was she going to spend the evening with Kelly, she was going to spend the evening with Kelly's date.

"I hope you have enough wine," Jo said as she pulled the first cork out.

Janis gave her shoulder a squeeze. "We have enough wine. You can have a whole bottle to yourself."

Jo glared at her, too.

Thankfully, Kerry and Shea arrived first, and Jo was spared seeing Kelly and her mystery date. And why did she even care? She had told Kelly that she would not go out with her, and she meant it. Emotionally, Kelly meant nothing to her. You could hardly say they were even friends. And if she had a date tonight, that was just fine with Jo. Maybe Kelly would quit pestering her about going out.

"Good to see you again, Jo," Shea told her.

"You, too. I guess we only run into each other at softball games."

Kerry grasped her shoulder tightly and Jo leaned away from the larger woman.

"We're having a backyard party next Saturday," Kerry said. "We'd like you to come. We're going to set up the volleyball net and we'll have barbecue and beer, of course."

"End of summer party," Shea added.

"Sounds like fun," Jo said. "Thanks."

Betsy left to answer the door while Jo silently prayed it was Kay knocking. She heard Kelly's husky laugh before she saw her, and Jo cursed her luck. Everyone was all smiles as they said hello to Kelly and. . . Lucy.

"Jo, isn't it?" Lucy asked as they shook hands.

"Yes," Jo said between gritted teeth. "Wine's in the kitchen. Let me get you a glass."

"No. I'll get us one."

Jo turned on Kelly as soon as Lucy was out of sight.

"No trouble getting a date?" she asked sweetly.

"Oh, gosh no," Kelly said. "Not with my reputation."

Jo glared at her as she followed Lucy into the kitchen. When Kay finally arrived, Jo was hardly in the mood to be civil.

"Have you met Toni?" Kay asked her.

"At the bar, yes." Jo shook her hand, again amazed at how young she looked. Kay had ended a relationship with a much older woman only months before Nancy skipped town. Since then, Kay rarely dated anyone older than thirty.

"Are you alone?" Kay asked.

"Of course," Jo said automatically. "Why muddle things up with a date?"

"Toni's got a roommate," Kay offered. "I think you would hit it off."

"A blind date? Be serious."

"She's a high school teacher," Toni chimed in.

"Great personality, too," Kay added.

Jo looked at Kay with raised eyebrows. "I appreciate your concern, but no," she said pointedly. She had enough trouble.

"Oh, Kelly and Lucy are here. Good," Kay said.

Good? Jo followed her gaze as Kelly and Lucy went with Betsy out to the deck. Through the double doors, she watched them talking, but turned away before Kelly caught her. It was as if Kelly could feel Jo's eyes on her, and Kelly had turned to search for her.

This has got to stop, Jo told herself. She purposefully turned her back to Kelly and listened as the others carried on a conversation without her. Once again, she was the fifth wheel, the only one without a date. The only one alone.

She knew immediately when Kelly came back into the room, she could feel her presence without turning around.

"I told Janis this wouldn't be a big deal, but I think we should sing," Betsy said and they laughed.

"Oh, wait," Jo said, handing her glass to Kay. "I almost forgot the cake."

"Cake?" Janis called. "You promised no cake, Johanna Marshall!"

Jo came back in with a cake disguised as two very large breasts. The groan from Janis was drowned out by everyone else's laughter when they read the greeting. "40. Eat 'em and weep!"

"Jo? How could you?" Janis demanded.

"Betsy made me," she laughed.

"Me?" Betsy cried with mock indignation.

"Good one, Jo," Kay said. "Let's light them."

They gathered around Janis and her breasts, and Jo held a match to the candles in each nipple.

“I’ll get you for this, Jo!” Janis warned.

They burst into an off-key version of “Happy Birthday” and Janis laughed delightfully during the entire song.

“Don’t give up your day jobs,” she teased before blowing out the two candles. She punched Jo playfully on the arm, then grabbed her for a quick hug. “Thank you,” she whispered.

Jo grinned, then went in search of more wine. She figured she would have a much easier time getting through the evening if she were drinking.

To her dismay, she was seated directly across from Kelly and Lucy, and she was forced to watch them during the entire meal. She tried to be discreet, but after her fourth glass of wine, she was staring. And to Kelly’s credit, she never gave any indication that she and Lucy were anything other than friends. Lucy, however, took every possible opportunity to touch Kelly. When they spoke, Lucy leaned close, practically rubbing her breasts on Kelly’s arm. Jo was disgusted!

She picked at her food, having to force down every bite, while trying to make polite conversation with Kay on her right and Shea on her left, but she found her eyes were always drawn to the couple across from her.

After cake, everyone started taking their leave, and Jo helped Betsy clear the table.

“One good thing about dinner parties,” Betsy said, “They don’t last all night.”

Ain’t it the truth, Jo silently agreed.

“Oh, that was fun,” Janis exclaimed, as she climbed on a barstool and watched Betsy and Jo clean up.

“I’m glad you liked it, honey,” Betsy said.

“The cake was evil,” she said and Jo laughed. “I’ll get you back,” she warned again.

“You’ll forget all about it by the time I’m forty.”

"Don't count on it!"

"Kelly was quiet tonight," Betsy observed.

"Yes, she was," Janis agreed.

Jo didn't comment. She and Kelly had not spoken, and the few times their eyes had met, it was almost as if they were strangers.

"I wonder if she and Lucy are seriously dating?" Betsy asked.

"I can't see it," Janis said. "Lucy just doesn't seem her type."

And what is her type? Jo wondered.

"Jo?"

Jo looked up, startled.

"You're quiet, too," Janis stated.

"Am I?" Jo hurried into the kitchen with her load of plates. "I'm just tired, I guess." It was an excuse that worked no matter what, and she didn't hesitate to use it now.

"We can get the rest, Jo. Don't worry about it," Betsy said from behind her.

"I know. I'm leaving." Then she grinned. "I'm sure you have a big night planned."

"Oh? Do we?" Janis asked innocently, and Betsy blushed.

Jo hugged both of them, and kissed Betsy on the cheek as she left. "Behave tonight," she teased. "You know Janis is getting old."

"I heard that!" Janis called after her.

Jo's smile vanished as soon as her car door slammed and the emptiness surrounded her. She didn't want to feel this way, and she cursed the day that Kelly Sambino came into her life. Her attraction to Kelly was undeniable, but she certainly didn't want it. She was getting along perfectly fine without her, thank you. Sure, she had been lonely sometimes. But never like this.

She imagined kissing Kelly, the taste of wine on Kelly's tongue, the feel of smooth skin beneath her fingertips. She shuddered. But it was too late. She drove home in a daze as Kelly came to her again and again, lips and tongue teasing her, tantalizing her. She offered her breast to Kelly, and soon a warm mouth closed over her. Jo moaned, the sound echoing in the quiet car, and she pushed her thoughts away.

But later, as she lay in her empty bed, she welcomed the images, and her eyes slid shut when Kelly's mouth came to her. She wanted to feel Kelly inside her. She wanted her fingers deep inside Kelly. She groaned and rolled over, tasting Kelly's skin beneath her mouth, feeling Kelly's nipples swell against her tongue.

She imagined it was Kelly's hand touching her now, caressing her breasts.

"Oh," she breathed when her fingers felt her own wetness. Her mouth opened, waiting for Kelly's kiss as her fingers moved, stroking herself, bringing herself closer to release.

It was Kelly's mouth on her, her tongue sliding into her, and finally her hips rose once, hard against her hand, and she turned her face into the pillow, stifling her scream.

When her breathing slowed to normal, Jo opened her eyes, half expecting Kelly to be there, watching her. But she was still alone. Still lonely.

Kelly was, no doubt, with Lucy.

Chapter Fifteen

Jo spent a lonely Sunday afternoon curled in the corner of her sofa, her thoughts jumping from the book in her lap to the football game on TV and finally to Kelly. She tried desperately to not think about last night. . . *Kelly with Lucy.*

Harry had some fishing buddies over so Jo had politely taken her leave after their earlier-than-usual brunch. She was actually looking forward to Monday. Maybe Kelly would forget about their conversation Friday and come into her office to talk. Maybe Jo could forget about the birthday party. She had been rude to Kelly, and really should apologize. But she never got the chance. Jo did not see Kelly all week.

The following Saturday, Jo decided to accept Kerry and Shea's invitation to their end of summer barbecue. They had insisted she come, or so Betsy said. Jo didn't really know them, but they were friends of Janis's. They had been a couple for fourteen years, and Janis had known them for six of those years. Of course, Jo knew she was only going in hopes of seeing Kelly. At least she could be honest with herself about that.

They lived in an old house in the Hyde Park area, with a huge backyard and a stone patio. A keg of beer was waiting, a barbecue pit was smoking, and the smell of smoking brisket assailed her when she walked up. A volleyball net was strung across the yard, and Betsy and Shea were serving to each other while the others argued over choosing sides. The entire softball team was supposed to be there. Johanna scanned the familiar faces, looking for Kelly.

Kelly finally showed, with Lucy in tow. Shocked, Jo stared at them, then quickly look away and finished filling her cup at the keg. Maybe they really were dating. It was obvious they had come together. Jo was knocked off balance by the pang of jealousy that hit her.

When sides were drawn for volleyball, Jo was thankful that she, Kelly and Lucy were on opposing teams. She played horribly, anyway. She never claimed to be an athlete, and she was, by far, the worst one there, what with all the softball players. To add to her disgust, Lucy turned out to be a fantastic jumper. Whenever she was on the front line, they scored, her spike invariably sailing between two players and smashing to the ground. Once, when Jo was playing opposite her, Lucy spiked the ball directly into Jo's face. Only by the grace of God did it not knock her out cold!

Jo went to the keg and drank two full cups of beer before she felt recovered. Thankfully, someone else showed up who took her place in the game.

She sat on the sideline with Janis, who refused to play. They watched as the others laughed and argued about out-of-bounds calls while Jo tried to keep her eyes off Kelly. But she couldn't and she finally stopped trying. There were more trips to the keg, spurred by the blatant attention Kelly was giving to Lucy. By the time the games were over and everyone else settled down in lawn chairs, Jo was well on her way to getting drunk.

"I've never seen you drink so much," Betsy said.

"Yeah, well, maybe I'm due a good hangover."

"At this rate, you won't be disappointed," she retorted.

"Stop. Please," Jo said.

"Okay. But maybe you need to think about why you're doing this."

Jo just stared at her and said nothing until Betsy shrugged and walked away.

Deb came and sat next to her, and Jo was more attentive than she should have been, but at least someone found her interesting. During dinner, Jo and Deb sat next to each other, and she nodded while Deb talked but she didn't really hear. She was too busy watching Kelly and Lucy sitting close together, talking quietly.

"Jo?"

Jo blinked several times, and brought her attention back to Deb.

"Sorry. What?"

"I said we never made our movie date. If you're that busy during the week, why don't we try for Friday or Saturday?"

Jo stared at Deb, who was clearly expecting a response. Her mind would not cooperate and no excuse miraculously came to her. Instead, she nodded weakly.

"Okay."

"Great! I'll call you later in the week and we'll plan it. Maybe we can have dinner, too." Deb was obviously thrilled and Jo cursed herself for being weak. She should just tell

Deb the truth, that she didn't want to go out with her. But she was getting very good at lying. An excuse would come later.

After the plates had been collected and everything cleaned up, they all settled again on the patio and Kerry put on soft music. Jo couldn't stand it. She walked slowly over to the keg to get another beer. She was surprised when Kelly walked up behind her.

"Are you trying to drink enough to pass out or what?" she asked.

Jo shot her an angry look. "Mind your own damn business."

Kelly ignored her remark and glanced at Deb. "I didn't realize that you and Deb were on such friendly terms."

Jo looked over at Lucy, then back at Kelly. "Yeah, well, same goes for you and Lucy."

"Hey, I figured I better start living up to my reputation," she shot back.

"Oh, and you've just now started?" Jo asked sarcastically.

"Actually, no, we've gone out a few times before."

Jo stared at her, her heart squeezing in her chest. "You have?" she whispered.

"Yes. She's fun to be around and she seems to like me as a person. She doesn't seem to believe my terrible reputation."

Jo felt as if she'd just been slapped. She suddenly felt like crying. "Have you slept with her?" she asked, so softly Kelly almost didn't hear.

She laughed harshly. "Why should you care?"

Jo raised her eyes, feeling tears stinging them. "I care," she whispered.

Kelly saw her tears and cursed. She looked down, then ran a hand through her hair. "God, what do you think I am?"

She shook her head, took the beer from Jo, set it down and led her inside the house where they could be alone.

"I haven't slept with her. I know you won't believe this, but I haven't been with anyone since that night in June," she said.

"You haven't?" Jo stared at her, then squeezed her eyes shut. She shouldn't care one way or the other. "I'm sorry. It's not any of my business what you do."

"No. It's not. I tried to make it your business, but you wouldn't let me."

"I know," she said quietly.

"What do you want from me?" Kelly asked softly.

"I want you to come by my office and ask me to lunch."

"So you can turn me down?"

Jo nodded.

Kelly smiled.

Jo felt like crying again.

"You've had too much to drink," Kelly said gently.

"It's your fault. I couldn't stand watching you with her. Not last Saturday. Not tonight."

"Are you jealous?"

Jo nodded. "But I have no right to be."

Kelly watched her for a long moment. "How are you getting home?"

"Betsy and Janis."

"Let me take you home," Kelly suggested.

Jo laughed. "I thought you were on a date."

"Lucy can find a ride home," she said. "Maybe with Deb."

"You're incorrigible," Jo said, shaking her head.

"It's not Lucy I want," Kelly said softly.

"Have you kissed her?" Jo asked, searching Kelly's face. "You have, haven't you?"

"Jo. . . ."

"Did you?" she whispered.

"Yes."

Jo was filled with such jealousy that it scared her. The thought of Kelly kissing someone else gripped painfully at her heart.

Kelly gathered her in her arms, and Jo wrapped her own around Kelly's waist, laying her head on her shoulder.

"So much for your reputation," Jo murmured.

"Goddamn it, Jo. It's not Lucy I want," she said again.

Jo pulled out of her arms. "But she wants you."

"And you don't," Kelly said.

Jo turned her back to Kelly and took a deep breath. "I do want you," she whispered.

"Jo?"

She turned back around and met Kelly's eyes. "I do want you," she repeated.

She no longer cared that she would hate herself in the morning. She no longer cared that Kelly was not the one for her. She wanted to make love with her again, and she could no longer deny herself that.

"Then let's get out of here."

"I'm going to hate myself tomorrow," Jo said.

"No," Kelly said softly and cupped her face with one palm. "I'll be right back. Stay here. I'll tell Lucy I'm leaving."

Jo wrapped her arms around herself, thinking she had lost her mind for agreeing to this. But for once, she wasn't going to talk herself out of it. It had been inevitable, after all.

Chapter Sixteen

Jo moved into Kelly's arms without thinking, their clothes having been shed as soon as the door shut behind them. She didn't want to know what Kelly had told the others, and Kelly didn't offer an explanation. It didn't matter, anyway. This was all that mattered.

"I've thought of this so often," Kelly whispered into her mouth.

"Yes, I have too," Jo admitted.

Jo led her to the bed and pulled Kelly down with her, their breasts touching, Kelly's mouth hot on her, her tongue delving deep, exploring. Her hands moved to Kelly's hair, fingers parting it, smoothing it, holding Kelly's face between her palms.

"I want you so much," Jo breathed.

"I'm yours," Kelly murmured against her lips.

They moved slowly, neither in a hurry, both wanting to prolong this pleasure. Kelly caressed Jo's face with soft fingers, then moved to her breasts, fingertips lightly grazing her taut nipples.

Jo laid her head back and closed her eyes, remembering the first time they had made love. It had been like this, too. Kelly's touch bringing all her senses to life, chest rising and falling, breath coming rapidly as she waited for Kelly's mouth to travel slowly from her lips, down her neck, to her breasts. Kelly's tongue touched her nipple, and she raised up to meet her as Kelly's mouth settled over one tip while her fingers caressed the other. She held her, letting Kelly have her fill. Kelly lifted up slightly and moved her mouth to the other breast, her legs shifting between Jo's. Jo pushed her hips up, her legs parting even wider.

Jo took Kelly's hand and placed it between them, forcing her to feel the wetness that she had caused, and she pressed her hand to her.

"Oh, God, look at you," Kelly whispered as her fingers found Jo's opening. Jo stifled a cry as Kelly's fingers parted her and delved into her, her hips rising to meet Kelly's thrusting fingers.

Kelly pulled her hand away and laid down full on top of Jo, their hips pressing together. Jo held her, her lips moving over Kelly's face before coming back to her mouth. Kelly moved down her body, trailing kisses as she went. Squirming and gasping in anticipation by the time Kelly's tongue moved to her inner thigh, Jo thought she would surely die if Kelly didn't hurry and take her.

"Please, I can't stand it."

She felt Kelly smile against her leg and then her mouth

moved the few inches as Jo rose up to meet her, laying back down as Kelly settled over her.

"Dear God," she breathed, and her fingers clutched Kelly's shoulders, holding her there for fear she would stop, but Kelly's mouth and tongue moved over her greedily, relentlessly, devouring her, opening her.

"Yes," Jo sighed, biting her lip and shutting her eyes tightly, feeling the sensation of Kelly's mouth wash over her. She had dreamed of this moment since that night in June. Her orgasm was building and her breath caught. All too soon her hips were thrusting forward and she was screaming out her pleasure and gasping as her body shuddered until Kelly's mouth finally stilled.

"Oh," she said softly and drew Kelly to her, folding her in her arms. "That was so wonderful."

Kelly's hands caressed her hair and soothed her while Jo's heart slowed and her breathing eased. She raised her head after awhile, and Jo kissed her mouth. "Lay back," Jo said quietly. Kelly released her and lay still, and Jo saw the rise and fall of her breasts. She put her lips there, tongue teasing a nipple before taking it into her mouth. She had always been so passive in bed, but she was different with Kelly. She wanted to please her, wanted her to forget all the countless others that had come before. Jo wanted her to remember only her.

Jo took Kelly's hands and pinned them above her head, then straddled her, her hips sinking down against Kelly. Their eyes held, and Jo lowered her mouth, kissing Kelly hard.

"I've wanted you for so long," she admitted. "I've dreamed of making love to you."

Jo cupped Kelly's breast and covered it with her mouth, sucking the nipple inside, her tongue caressing the hard peak. Jo raised her hips, just enough to slip her hand between their bodies. When her fingers touched Kelly's wetness, Jo groaned, and bit gently at Kelly's nipple. Jo slipped first one, then two fingers inside Kelly. She pulled out slowly, only to delve back deep inside her. Kelly's hips rocked against Jo's hand, and Jo sat up, watching Kelly's face contort in concentration. Jo matched Kelly's rhythm, her fingers moving deeper with each thrust.

"Yes," Kelly breathed. "Faster."

But there wasn't time. Seconds later, Kelly screamed, a deep, primal scream that thrilled Jo to her very core. She withdrew slowly, fingers wet, she wiped them against Kelly's breast, only to put her mouth there.

"I want my mouth on you," Jo murmured. "I want to taste you."

"Jo. . . I can't. Give me a second." Kelly tried to pull Jo to her, but Jo resisted.

"I just want to taste you."

Jo moved down, wetting Kelly's side, her stomach, with her tongue. Jo's hands pushed Kelly's legs apart and she trailed kisses over Kelly's hips and thighs, into the hollows at her knees, then back up. Kelly lay still as Jo caressed her leg, down to her smooth calf, then back up again.

Jo smiled when she felt Kelly's hands grip her shoulders to push her down, to guide her. Jo breathed deeply, Kelly's scent arousing her even more, and her mouth went to the source of her pleasure, tasting her, feeling the silky wetness with her tongue. Kelly pushed up, then lay back down as Jo stroked her quickly. She was smooth and soft and oh, so wet, and Jo nearly devoured her, bringing her to orgasm quickly. Kelly surged up, and Jo felt Kelly's fingers dig into her shoulders as she cried out.

"Oh, dear God," she whispered. Kelly lay back, her arms again limp at her sides, and Jo kissed her gently.

"You're such a beautiful lover," Kelly sighed, and gathered Jo up beside her.

Jo smiled, her hand gently cupping Kelly's breast. She couldn't seem to stop touching her, and she tried not to think about how much she still wanted her.

Their lovemaking took them well into the morning when, exhausted, they finally fell asleep in each other's arms.

Chapter Seventeen

Jo opened her eyes slowly, half-afraid that Kelly would be gone again, but she was sound asleep beside her. Jo watched Kelly sleep, her face smooth and dark, her brown hair tousled from Jo's hands. Jo's gaze settled on Kelly's lips, still swollen from their kisses. She watched her for a long moment, refusing to think about what she had done last night, remembering only the sweet lovemaking they had shared and the ecstasy this woman had brought to her.

She finally reached to touch Kelly's lips with her own. Kelly moved under the covers and stretched, her eyes still closed. A small smile formed on her lips, then her eyes opened, and she found Jo staring at her.

"Good morning," she murmured.

"Mmm," Jo nodded and propped her head up on her palm.

"Is everything okay?" Kelly asked gently.

"Yes. I'm just watching you."

Kelly smiled and found Jo's breast under the covers. "You can watch me all you want."

"Breakfast?"

"You can cook, too?"

"Pancakes?"

"And scrambled eggs?"

"Are you hungry?"

"Starving."

Jo was just starting breakfast when the phone rang, and though she thought about letting the machine get it, she picked it up on the third ring.

"Jo?"

"Yes."

"It's Deb."

Jo glanced guiltily down the hall, as if Deb could hear Kelly in the shower.

"Good morning," she said.

"How are you?"

"I'm fine," Jo said.

"Kelly said you were feeling ill last night. You should have said something, I would have taken you home."

Ill? What kind of ill? Why hadn't she bothered asking Kelly what she had said to them? Because she was too concerned with what they were about to do, that's why!

"Thank you, Deb. I just had too much to drink, and I was feeling a little queasy. Kelly insisted that she take me home."

"Well, it just seemed strange, her leaving poor Lucy there."

"I suppose." Jo didn't know what Deb expected her to say. Poor Lucy?

"I hope she didn't try anything," Deb said.

"I don't know what you mean," Jo said quietly.

"Lucy's told me how she is. How she goes out all the time, even though they've been dating since the summer. She even hits on women in front of Lucy."

Oh, God, Jo thought. She didn't need to hear this so early this morning, not after last night.

"They've been dating since summer?" she asked weakly.

"Oh, yes. I thought you knew. Lucy's head-over-heels in love. Kelly treats her this way and Lucy still wants to move in with her. Go figure."

Move in with her? Jo felt sick to her stomach. Kelly had lied to her. After last night, Jo had decided that she had been wrong about Kelly, that her reputation was undeserved. But it was like Nancy all over again, the lies she told, the stories Jo would hear from her friends. When was she going to learn? She had known from the beginning that Kelly was no good for her. She had known about her reputation and still, she had let herself be fooled into thinking that she was not like Nancy.

"Had I known that she and Lucy were so involved, I would never have accepted a ride from her. I hope Lucy doesn't think it was my idea." Actually, Jo could not care less what Lucy thought.

"I'm just glad you're okay and she didn't try anything."

"I'm fine," Jo lied.

"Well, she's very attractive," Deb continued. "I can see how someone could be swayed by her."

Swayed? Is that what had happened last night?

"I've got to go, Deb. I'm going to Harry's and he's expecting me. Thanks for calling."

She hung up without waiting for Deb's reply and gripped the countertop hard, her eyes shut tight against the threatening tears. How could she have been so foolish? When would she ever learn?

"Jo?"

Jo kept her back to Kelly while she tried to get herself under control. She would not let Kelly see her cry!

"What's wrong?"

"That was Deb," she said.

"Deb?"

"On the phone."

"I didn't hear it ring," Kelly said.

Jo turned around slowly, but she refused to meet Kelly's eyes.

"How long have you been sleeping with Lucy?"

"What?" She stared at her, lines breaking her smooth brow into a frown. "I've not slept with her. I already told you that."

"Deb says that you've been dating since summer."

"Is that why she called?"

"She called to see how I was. She's a friend," Jo said.

"And in asking how you were, she just happened to mention that Lucy and I had been seeing each other?"

"Something like that," Jo said. "She was concerned that you might have forced yourself on me."

"And did I?" Kelly asked.

"No," Jo admitted, finally daring to meet her eyes.

Kelly walked into the kitchen and stood in front of Jo and held her gaze tightly. "Lucy and I went out a few times when I first moved here, but I never slept with her. I could have. She didn't exactly make it a secret that she wanted to. But I swear, we've been nothing but friends."

Jo said nothing, but she didn't look away.

"How can you believe that?" Kelly asked, her dark eyes piercing Jo's.

"I refused to believe it with Nancy, even after Betsy and Janis said they had seen her with this other woman. I didn't listen to my friends at the beginning, either. Nancy came with a long list of exes and a reputation fit for the gutter, but I wouldn't listen."

"I'm not Nancy."

"No? Well, maybe I just don't want to be another notch on your belt," Jo said.

"After everything that happened last night, you'd believe that? Hell, maybe I should go check your headboard. You probably have notches all over it. After all, you're the one who brought me here. Twice, now," she said angrily.

Jo stared at her, feeling as if she'd been slapped. "How dare you say that?"

"Oh? Do we have different rules for me?"

"That's not what I meant," Jo said.

"Jo, wake up! Did it ever occur to you that Deb may have an ulterior motive?"

"Like what?"

"She likes you. She wants you. You'd have to be blind not to see that. Do you think she didn't know something was going on with us last night? That's the only reason she called."

"You're wrong. She doesn't like me that way. We've been friends for too long. She wouldn't lie to me," Jo insisted.

"But I would?"

Jo stared at her, not knowing what to say. Her silence said it all, however.

"I can't believe you," Kelly whispered. "If you want to think that last night meant nothing, that it was just about sex, well, that's fine."

She walked away from Jo, then stopped. "I guess you're

right. There's not anything between us. My mistake for thinking that there could be," she said bitterly. "You've got to have trust in a relationship, any kind of a relationship, and we don't have that. I'm not so certain any more that we can even be friends, much less lovers."

Jo saw the hurt in her eyes as she walked to the door.

"Kelly, don't leave like this," Jo pleaded.

"Why? There's nothing else to say, Johanna." Their eyes met. "I'm not one of the bad guys, but I can't make you believe that," she said softly.

"I didn't say that you were, but Nancy hurt me more than I care to remember. I can't take that chance again."

"I'm not Nancy. I've never cheated on anyone."

They stared at each other in silence, both weighing the words between them.

"I'm truly sorry, Jo."

Their eyes held for a moment longer and Jo saw how terribly hurt Kelly was, but she didn't stop her from walking out the door. She wouldn't allow herself.

She stood in the kitchen for a long time after Kelly drove away, then made herself move. She refused to acknowledge the pain that she had seen in Kelly's eyes and that she was the one who had put it there. It was better to end it now.

She called Harry later that afternoon and invited him out to dinner.

"Why don't you come over here, Jo-Jo? I've got some ribs soaking in a marinade. I was going to put them on the smoker."

"Okay. I'll be over by five."

They spent the evening together, and Jo was pleased that Harry seemed to be in a good mood. He talked nonstop and didn't seem to notice how quiet Jo was until she was getting ready to go.

"Tell me what's wrong, Jo-Jo," he said, startling her.

"Nothing, Harry."

"Don't lie to your grandfather, girl," he said sternly.

"My personal life sucks," she finally admitted, drawing a smile from him.

"This woman you've met?" he asked.

She nodded. "Kelly."

"And?"

"I like her, but she's not right for me."

"What's not right?"

"She's too much like Nancy," she said. But was she really? "With a reputation like hers, anyway."

"I don't think you need to get involved with someone like Nancy, Jo-Jo." He looked at her. "But you're already involved?"

Jo nodded. "She's nothing like Nancy, really." She shrugged. "Maybe I'm being unfair, comparing them. It's just that I was so hurt."

"I know, sweetheart." He hugged her to him. "You'll know if it's right or not."

"I guess so."

"So, what's she say about it?"

"She says the things I've heard aren't true. I hurt her today."

Harry nodded. "That's not good," he added softly. "I can tell you're upset about it."

"It's just that I've heard things about her."

"Well, you've got to learn to weed out the truth. Sometimes people say things about others for a reason and it's not always true. If you like her, you need to give her some benefit of the doubt."

"You think so?"

"Yes."

"I really do love you," she said and kissed his cheek.

"I love you, too, Jo-Jo."

Chapter Eighteen

Jo let her class before lunch go early and hurried to her office, afraid she might miss a chance to see Kelly. She needed to tell her she was sorry for what she had said. Harry was right. She needed to give her a chance. But Kelly didn't come into her office at twelve-thirty. Jo wasn't really surprised. What had she expected? She had accused her of being a cheat and a liar, not to mention a collector of women! If Kelly never forgave her for that, Jo couldn't blame her.

That night, lying in bed, she closed her eyes and remembered Kelly beside her, touching her. Jo had never enjoyed lovemaking as much as she had the two nights she had been with Kelly. They had a spark between them. When they touched, it was explosive.

She mentally shook herself. She did not need this drama in her life. Christy would have no reason to lie, even if Deb and Lucy did. She couldn't very well call Lucy up and ask her if they had slept together. It was really none of her business. And Deb, she refused to believe that Deb would lie to her. They were friends. After all this time, why would Deb show a romantic interest in her? But Deb had danced too close that night at the bar. Jo closed her eyes, trying to organize her thoughts as they came tumbling down around her. She was going in circles with her feelings. One minute, she thought she should take a chance with Kelly. The next minute, never.

She did not see Kelly until the following afternoon when she was just returning to her office after her last class. Kelly was heading down the hall with her arms full of books and papers.

"Hey," Kelly said and stopped.

"Hi."

"How are you?" she asked.

Jo noticed there was no smile in her eyes and none on her face. "I'm okay," Jo replied.

"Good. Listen, I'm running late. I'll see you around," she said and hurried off.

"Sure," Jo called after her but Kelly was already out the door at the end of the hall.

"Sure," she said again, to herself.

Jo walked to her office, sat down and stared at the papers on her desk. Her assistant had been busy, she noted. She didn't care. She shoved the papers aside and rested her elbows there instead, holding her head. She missed Kelly, but it was her own fault. This was the way she had said she wanted it.

On Wednesday, Kelly was nowhere to be found, and by the afternoon, Jo went in search of her. Her office was locked and Jo went to find Susan.

"I haven't seen her today," Jo explained.

"Oh, she's here somewhere," Susan said, absently shuffling papers on her desk. "I think she has a friend in from out of town, though."

A friend? Who? Jo willed Susan to continue, but she didn't, so Jo left her to her work and slowly made her way back to her office. She had mounds of work to do herself, but she didn't have the heart. Instead, she called Harry and invited herself over to dinner.

"Jo-Jo, I'm sorry. We're having a dinner at the Senior Center tonight."

"Oh."

"I can always cancel," he offered.

"No, don't be silly," she said.

"Why don't you come over for lunch on Saturday? It's supposed to be beautiful weather. Maybe we'll take the boat out."

She smiled and agreed. "I'll be there in the morning," she said as she hung up.

On Thursday, when Kelly again did not come to her office, Jo walked down the hall to her open door. Kelly was typing rapidly on the computer but raised her head when Jo walked in. Their eyes met for a split second then Kelly looked back to the terminal.

"What's up?" she asked as she typed.

"I just haven't seen you all week," Jo said.

Kelly's hands paused over the keyboard. "Did you think you would?" she asked.

Jo was taken aback by her words. "I thought maybe we needed to talk," she said.

Kelly looked at her briefly, then went on typing. "I've been busy and no, I don't think we have anything to talk about," she finally said.

"Susan said you had a friend in," Jo said, before she could stop herself.

Kelly looked up again. "Yes, I do."

She didn't offer more, and Jo didn't dare ask.

"Well, I'll leave you to your work, then."

Jo cursed herself all the way back to her office and slammed her door once she got there. "Damn the woman," she said aloud.

Jo had sent Kelly away, yet she was miserable. She sat around daily thinking of Kelly, wondering what she was doing. And with whom.

She did not see Kelly at all on Friday. Her class was surprised when she again let them leave early, but the truth was, she just could not stand another minute there. She had to get away.

That night, she went out to dinner with Betsy and Janis. They went to Bonita's, and she was again reminded of the first night she had been with Kelly. She cursed herself for her thoughts. Let it go, she told herself.

"How's Kelly?" Betsy asked.

"I imagine fine," Jo said.

"You imagine?"

"I haven't seen her much this week," Jo said.

"Really?" Janis said, and her tone indicated to Jo that she knew they hadn't been seeing each other.

"Why not?" Betsy asked bluntly.

"Look, just how much do you know?" Jo finally asked.

Betsy put her fork down. "We know about that night in June. We know about last weekend. We know you told her to get lost," she said.

"She told you?" Jo asked, her eyes wide.

"Well, yes," Janis said. "We've talked."

"Actually, we had dinner with her this week," Betsy said.

"You have? I didn't realize you were such good friends."

"Well, we do go to all the softball games," Janis said. "We've become friends."

"She's not a bad person, Jo," Betsy added.

"How do you know that?" she asked. "Do you really know her?"

"Jo, you can't compare everyone to Nancy," Betsy said.

"I don't compare everyone to Nancy. But Betsy," she said, leaning forward. "let's face it, Kelly comes with a reputation, just like Nancy did. Almost worse, in fact."

"An offhand remark from Christy doesn't count. And you can't believe what Deb told you. Hell, she's got the hots for you. She'd say anything to get you."

"Deb does not have the hots for me, as you so crudely put it."

"Of course she does. Why are you the only one who can't see it?" Betsy shook her finger at Jo playfully. "And don't think Deb didn't know something was up with you and Kelly that night. Why else would she call you and fill your head with crap about Lucy?"

"Kelly told you that, too?"

"Yes, she told us everything," Janis said. "She needed to talk. She was hurt and upset." Janis lowered her voice. "She really cares for you."

"I don't want her to care for me," Johanna said stubbornly. "I can't go through that again."

They were silent for a moment, then Betsy picked up her taco again. "Well, you don't have to worry about that now, do you?" She took a bite of her dinner. "I think things are over between you two, anyway. Right?"

Jo didn't answer, just gazed thoughtfully at her friends. Yes, things were over, if they had ever even started.

Chapter Nineteen

Jo slept late on Saturday morning, then took time to start laundry before going to Harry's. It was a beautiful November day, just like he had predicted, and she was looking forward to spending the day at the lake. She vowed she would not think of Kelly today, although she had had a restless night thinking about her. Surely, she could get through the day without doing the same.

She listened to her favorite Elton John CD on the way to Harry's, driving with the sunroof open. Clear, blue skies overhead helped to brighten her mood and by the time she drove down Harry's driveway, she was singing.

Parking in her usual spot she was surprised Harry was not sitting on the porch waiting for her, like he usually did.

She had picked up some things for their lunch, and she grabbed the sack from the seat beside her.

The front door was open and she went in.

"Harry?" she called.

There was no sound in the house, and she assumed he had gone to the boathouse. She went into the kitchen and frowned. His breakfast dishes were still out, pans still on the stove. It was very unlike him to leave a mess. Putting the food she had brought in the refrigerator, she looked around, hands on her hips and then walked into the living room, thinking he must be outside. She looked out on the deck and saw him.

"Harry!" she screamed as she ran to the door and threw it open.

He was lying on the deck, his coffee cup shattered on the boards beside him.

"Oh, God, no," she pleaded. She bent to him and heard his shallow breathing. Without hesitating, she ran back inside, dialed 911, requested an ambulance and then hurried back to his side.

His hands were cold when she held them. "Harry, please," she begged. "Don't you dare leave me."

It seemed like hours before she heard the sirens. She didn't know what to do for him so she sat beside him on the deck, in spite of the broken glass, holding his hand and stroking his face, talking softly to him.

When the ambulance finally pulled up, she ran to the front door and called to them.

"Back here!" she yelled.

They were on the deck in no time, gently moving her aside so they could get to Harry. "Just stand back, ma'am. We'll take care of him."

She leaned against the railing, one hand covering her mouth as she watched them take his vital signs and give him oxygen. They spoke in low tones, and she couldn't make out all they were saying.

"Ma'am, we're going to take him over to Breckenridge. You can ride with us," the young man told her and she nodded numbly, following as they carried Harry away.

She sat in the emergency room for a full hour and a half before she heard anything. She thought she should call Betsy but she didn't want to leave, even for a minute.

"Ms. Marshall?" a woman asked from the doorway.

"Here," Johanna said, rising.

"I'm Dr. Stewart," she said, and offered Johanna a smile. Jo took her outstretched hand but did not return her smile.

"How is he?" she asked. She had no patience for pleasantries.

"Let's sit down," the doctor suggested, motioning to the uncomfortable chair that Jo had been sitting in.

"He's had a stroke," she began.

"Oh, no," Jo gasped.

"I'm afraid he's in a coma, Ms. Marshall. His vital signs are very weak. I'm worried about his heart. This has put a tremendous stress on his system, especially at his age."

"What are you saying?" Jo whispered.

She smiled, but Jo could tell it was forced. "I just want you to be prepared. He had what is called a cerebral embolism, resulting in severe trauma to the brain. The next 48 hours will be critical. We've relieved as much pressure as possible, but now we just have to wait."

Jo rubbed her forehead wearily. "Can I see him?" she asked.

"You can sit with him for just a moment," Dr. Stewart said. "Come with me."

Johanna followed her to the Intensive Care Unit. All around were the sounds and smells of the sick and dying, and she squeezed back her tears as she looked in on Harry. He was very pale, his snow white hair blending with the sheets. He had tubes in his nose and mouth, helping him breathe, she supposed. She walked slowly to him and took his cool, limp hand.

"Oh, Harry," she whispered.

"I'll have a nurse bring you a chair, Ms. Marshall."

"Thank you," she murmured, without turning around. Her eyes were fixed on Harry's face, which looked so smooth and peaceful. What was he thinking? About Beth?

A nurse brought a chair for her, and she sat down beside his bed, holding his hand, trying to warm it. She looked up at the monitor above his head, keeping track of the slow beat of his heart, and wept.

"Don't leave me, Harry," she cried softly. "I'm not sure I can make it without you."

Tears rolled down her face and she wiped them away absently. Her mind flashed back to some of their times together. She thought about the first summer she had lived with him and Beth, after her mother had been killed. He had taught her to drive the boat that summer, and they had spent endless days fishing and swimming in the lake. The next summer, he had taught her to drive his old Ford pickup, a four-speed with a temperamental clutch. He had stood beside her throughout high school, when she had run wild and nearly drove her grandmother insane, and he had proudly watched as she graduated college a few years later. All those years, he had taken care of her and protected her. Now, what could she do to repay him?

"Nothing," she whispered. "I can't do anything for you." She hung her head and sobbed, holding his hand to her face. "Oh, Harry."

She stayed at the hospital until nine that night, sitting with him for a few minutes at a time. Just before nine, a nurse touched her gently on the shoulder and told her it was time for her to go.

"When can I come back?"

"In the morning," she said kindly.

Jo nodded and walked away, turning back once to look at him again. She stood in the parking lot and looked at the sky, trying to decide what to do. She should call Betsy, and his friends from the Senior Center. But even that was too much effort. Instead, she hailed one of the cabs lining the circle drive and sat mutely as she was driven back to the lake.

The silence at his house was nearly her undoing. He should be here, she thought. She occupied herself by cleaning his kitchen and sweeping up the broken glass on the deck, but it was so quiet in the house, she couldn't stand it. She locked up quickly and drove home, dazed.

Once home, she knew what she needed to do. Without thinking, she picked up the college directory, found Kelly's number and punched it out quickly. It was Saturday and late, and she wondered for one awful second what she would do if Kelly wasn't home. Or worse, if she wasn't alone.

Kelly picked up on the third ring and just the sound of her voice brought a fresh sob from Jo.

"Kelly?"

"Jo? What is it?" she asked, concern in her voice.

"I need you," she said softly, her own voice cracking.

"What's wrong?"

"It's Harry," she sobbed.

"What happened, Jo?"

"He had a stroke. He's in the hospital."

"I'm so sorry," Kelly said gently.

"I need you tonight," Jo whispered.

"I'm on my way," she said and hung up.

A few minutes later, Kelly walked in and found Jo huddled in the corner of her sofa, her knees drawn up to her chest. Jo looked at up her, then let out her breath, sobs shaking her shoulders. Kelly sat beside her and drew her into her arms. Jo cried for a long time while Kelly softly stroked her hair, wiped her tears as they fell, and kissed her forehead gently.

"He's all I have in the whole world," Jo cried.

"Go ahead and cry. I'm here for you, Jo" Kelly said softly, and Jo cried harder.

"He's not even trying to fight this. He's missed my grandmother so much."

"What do the doctors say?"

"He's in a coma. They don't think he'll make it," she said, burying her face in Kelly's shoulder and sobbing.

"I'm so sorry." Kelly held her close, stroking her hair until Jo had cried herself out.

"Come on. I'll help you to bed. You need to sleep some, you'll have a long day tomorrow."

Jo let herself be guided down the hall and into her bedroom like a child. She stood silently as Kelly pulled back the covers on her bed.

"What else can I do for you?" she asked.

"Oh, Kelly, please don't go. Please stay with me," Jo said and swallowed another sob.

"I don't think I should," Kelly said.

"Please."

"Okay. I'll sleep out on the sofa."

Jo hung her head and felt fresh tears fall down her cheeks. She doesn't want me anymore, she thought.

"What is it?" Kelly asked gently.

"I need you," Jo said through her tears.

"I'm here."

Jo shook her head. "I need you to hold me, to touch me," she whispered.

"Oh, honey," Kelly said softly and went to her.

Jo wrapped her arms around Kelly's waist and held her tightly as Kelly's arms enfolded her, holding her close.

"I'll stay with you. Come, lie down." Kelly led her to the bed, and Jo sat on the edge and let Kelly undress her. Then she crawled under the covers. Kelly turned out the light, shed her clothes, and finally Jo felt her weight settle on the bed beside her.

"Come here." Kelly pulled Jo into her arms and held her, her hand brushing the hair from Jo's eyes. "You'll be okay," she whispered.

Jo laid her head on Kelly's shoulder, cheek pressed against her breast, and felt safe. Her eyes closed wearily, and relaxed as Kelly's soft hands caressed her back she finally fell asleep.

Later she woke with a start, still in Kelly's arms, nestled at her side. Her neck ached. She looked at the digital clock. Three-fifteen.

"What is it?" Kelly asked sleepily.

"Nothing." She sat up and moved Kelly's arm down to her side. "Your arm must be asleep by now."

"What arm?" Kelly asked and flexed it.

Jo was suddenly aware of their nakedness, and she settled back down, curling up beside Kelly again. Her hand moved under the covers and cupped Kelly's breast, her thumb rubbing Kelly's nipple lightly, feeling it harden against her fingers.

"Jo?" Kelly breathed.

"I want you," Jo whispered.

"Jo, don't," Kelly warned.

"Don't you want me anymore?" she asked.

"You know I do."

"Then make love to me," Jo insisted. "I need you." She raised up and found Kelly's mouth, kissing her tenderly.

"Yes," Kelly breathed and pulled her close.

Their lovemaking was quick and frantic, then slow and gentle as they took pleasure in each other's arms. This was what Jo needed, what she wanted. She wouldn't send her away again.

Chapter Twenty

Jo woke at seven and sniffed the air, smelling breakfast. She sat up, thankful that Kelly had not left. She wasn't ready to be alone. She walked naked into the bathroom and took a quick shower before finding Kelly in the kitchen.

She was at the sink washing dishes when Jo walked in. She glanced over her shoulder and their eyes met.

"Good morning," Kelly said and turned back to the sink.

Jo walked up to her and hugged her around the waist, pressing her breasts against Kelly's back. Kelly turned around then and held her with wet, soapy hands.

"Thank you for being here when I needed you," Jo said quietly.

"I want to be here for you, if you'll let me."

Jo pulled away and looked at her. "I've just been so awful to you. Why do you keep coming back?"

Kelly smiled. "If I told you the truth, it would send you running again."

Jo looked closely and saw the answer to her question in Kelly's dark eyes. Jo was frightened by what she saw there. She was glad that Kelly said nothing. She didn't want to hear the words. She wasn't ready yet.

"I hope you don't mind," Kelly said, motioning to the stove where bacon sat draining on a paper towel. "You probably don't feel like eating, but it's going to be a long day."

"I know. But I am hungry."

"Good. Why don't you call the hospital and I'll start on the eggs."

"Okay." The reality of the day was catching up to her. "Over easy," Jo requested and walked into the living room.

She found the number to the hospital and waited for the nurse in Intensive Care to pick up.

"I'm Johanna Marshall, Harry Marshall's granddaughter. Has there been any change?" she asked, holding her breath.

"No. I'm sorry, Ms. Marshall. There's no change."

"Okay. Thanks. I'll be there later this morning."

Kelly stuck her head in. "Well?" she asked.

"No change," she said, holding her gaze.

Kelly walked over and held her. "No change is better than a change for the worse," she said, and Jo nodded.

Jo really wasn't hungry anymore, but she forced down the bacon, eggs and toast Kelly had made. She hadn't eaten since breakfast the day before, and she knew she needed more than just coffee.

"I need to call Betsy," Jo said. "And Susan."

"Don't worry about it. I'll call them," Kelly offered.

"Thanks, that would help."

"Do you want me to take you to the hospital?"

"Oh, no. I'll be fine," she said. "You've done enough."

Then she remembered the friend Kelly had staying with her. "Do you have company?" Jo asked her.

Kelly nodded. "Yeah, I do."

"Now? At your place?"

"Yeah. But I called her this morning."

"Oh," Jo said quietly.

"Jo, she's an old friend from college."

"You don't have to explain to me," Jo said.

"I do have to explain. I can see what you're thinking. Kim and I roomed together in the dorm our freshman year and have been friends ever since. Just friends. She's got a girlfriend, they've been together ten years or more." Kelly met her eyes. "She just came to visit, honest."

"I believe you," Jo said and she did.

"I'm not like what you think," Kelly said softly.

"No, I don't think you are. You came to me last night without a question. I needed you so much," she admitted.

"I'm glad it was me you needed."

They smiled across the table as Kelly took her hand. "Everything will be fine."

Jo was at the hospital at just a few minutes past nine. Harry looked the same as when she had left him, pale and still. Her chair had been moved against the wall, and she pulled it over by his side and took his cool hand in hers.

"Good morning, Harry," she whispered. "It's a beautiful day out. Perfect for boat riding." She willed her tears away and continued. "You know, you promised me a boat ride yesterday."

He was perfectly still, his hand limp in hers.

"Oh, Harry. I need to talk to you," she said, wiping at

a tear that had escaped. "Remember I told you about Kelly? How she was no good for me? Well, I'm not so sure anymore. She was with me last night when I needed her, and this morning. I like her a lot, Harry. More than I should, I know. And, God, I think she's in love with me.

"She didn't say it, thank goodness, because I don't know what I would have done. I'm certainly not ready for that."

She reached up and touched his face, ignoring the tubes attached to him. "You always said that you didn't want to leave me alone. I wish you could meet her. You've always been such a good judge of character. I know you'd be able to tell me if she's the one for me, Harry. I just don't know. I don't know if I can let her get close, though. If something happened, I would need you there to help me get through it."

She let her tears come. She couldn't fight them anymore. "Oh, Harry, please don't leave me," she pleaded. "I need you."

She held his hand tightly, then brought her face to rest in his palm. "I love you."

Betsy and Janis came before lunch and stayed with her for an hour.

"We can stay longer," Betsy insisted.

"No, there's nothing for you to do here. I'll call if there's any change," Jo assured them.

A group from the Senior Center came, too, and Jo thanked them. It was nice to know he had friends there. At two, she walked to the cafeteria to get a sandwich, which she had to force down. She couldn't seem to think of anything except Harry, and she felt so helpless. And hopeless.

Later that afternoon, while she sat with him, she felt his hand twitch in hers, and she looked closely at him, praying that his eyes would open and he would smile at her and call her Jo-Jo.

"Harry?" She gripped his hand tightly, wanting to feel him move again, but then she noticed the monitor over his head. His even heartbeat was no longer showing. Instead, one steady line ran across the screen.

"Oh, no!" she cried. "No, Harry!" She held his hand to her face and cried, her shoulders shaking with sobs.

She was shoved out of the way as the doctors went to him and a nurse ushered her out of his room. "Ms. Marshall, please, let us take care of him," she said gently.

Jo couldn't move. Tears streamed down her face, and she couldn't pull her eyes away. She knew that if she did, she would never see him again.

No," she cried, shaking her head.

"Come, you must." The nurse insisted, and Jo turned slowly away, sobs coming with great force, shaking her slender shoulders.

"Good-bye, Harry," she whispered and covered her face with her hands. She left without looking back. She didn't want to see what they did to him. She walked blindly out the door and to her car, where she sat and cried.

Without thinking, she drove to his house. She wanted to be close to him and this was where he was. She walked down to the dock and started the boat, unmindful of the cool evening approaching. Speeding along the lake, she let the wind dry her tears as fast as they fell. She eased up on the throttle when she came upon a flock of ducks, then idled slowly as the waves rocked the boat. The coots had returned, she noted, seeing several mixed in with the ducks. Harry used to curse the coots, or mud hens, as he called them. He claimed they would come by the hundreds and rob his birdfeeders. She teased that he never should have started feeding them. She knew he secretly enjoyed watching them, the way they seemed to run across the water when startled.

They were as familiar during the winter months as the robins that returned each fall.

She leaned against the side of the boat and waved her hands wildly over her head. On cue, the coots took off, their feet striking the water as they ran out of harm's way. The mallards simply cocked their heads, dismissing her crazy antics.

"That was for Harry!" she yelled at the coots. Then, feeling foolish, she turned the boat around. The sun had set, but she wasn't worried. She knew the lake like the back of her hand and followed the shoreline home.

She was chilled when she got back. Dusk was upon her and she made her way to the dark house, following the familiar path she and Harry had walked for years.

Taking down his bottle of scotch, she poured herself a liberal amount and sat in his chair in the living room, sipping slowly. She felt numb. She had cried herself dry. Staring out over the lake, she watched the water ripple in the glare of the boathouse light. Occasionally, a boat sped past, and she watched its lights fade in the darkness.

Finally, she made herself get up and go home. Tomorrow, she would have to be strong. Tomorrow, she would have to make arrangements for Harry, and she dreaded it. She had done it all when Beth had died, Harry had been too distraught. Now, there was no one to take care of the details for her, however distraught she may be.

Her answering machine was blinking when she walked into the living room, and she pushed the "play" button as she walked past.

"Jo? Are you there?" Kelly's soft voice sounded urgent to her ears. "I called the hospital. I'm so sorry, honey. Please, call me when you get home."

She felt her heart tighten at Kelly's words, and she bit her lip.

The next message was from Betsy. "Kelly just called us. Where are you? Do you need us to come over? Why don't you come stay with us tonight? Call me, please."

Jo nodded to the machine and listened to the next message. It was from Kelly again. "Jo, where are you? Please call me. I'm worried about you."

Jo walked to the phone and dialed Kelly's number as another message from her played. "Jo, goddamn it, if you're there, pick up the phone. Don't shut me out, please."

Kelly answered on the first ring.

"It's me," Jo said quietly.

"Where have you been?"

"At the lake."

"I'm coming over," Kelly insisted.

"Yes, please," Jo said, and Kelly hung up without saying good-bye.

Next, she called Betsy. "Yes, I'm okay."

"Do you want to come over?"

"No. Kelly's coming here."

"Good. You don't need to be alone, Jo. God, I'm so sorry, honey. I know how close you were."

"Yes, I'll miss him," she whispered.

"What can we do?" Betsy asked.

"I don't know yet. Tomorrow I'll think about the funeral. Tonight, I just want to forget."

"I understand. I'll come over tomorrow, okay?" Betsy asked.

"Yes, I'd be grateful," Jo sighed.

She was making herself a drink when Kelly drove up. She walked in without knocking.

"Jo?" she called.

"I'm in the kitchen," Jo called back.

Kelly walked in, took her in her arms and held her close.

"I was so worried about you," she whispered. "Why didn't you call someone?"

"I just didn't think, I guess." Jo felt the tears forming again. "I can't believe he's gone," she cried.

"Shhh. I know, honey. I'm so sorry you had to go through that alone. I wish I could have been there for you."

Jo was touched by her words and sobbed on Kelly's shoulder. It felt so good to be held, so good to feel loved. She pulled away and raised red, tired eyes to Kelly. "Please, will you stay with me tonight?"

"Of course," Kelly said gently. "I'll take care of you."

Jo remembered Harry hoping that she'd have someone to take care of her, and she wished now that he could know she did have someone.

Jo slept soundly that night in Kelly's arms and didn't wake until nearly seven. Kelly was still with her, though awake and watching her.

"How long have you been awake?" Jo asked, her voice hoarse from crying.

"Just a little while," she said softly.

"You've got to get to school," Jo said.

"Yeah, I know. I hate to leave you, though."

"I'll be okay. I've done this before," she said flatly.

"You shouldn't have to do it alone," Kelly pulled Jo near.

"I'll be okay," she repeated.

Kelly kissed her tenderly. "I've got to get going. I have to go by my place for clothes."

"It's okay. Go," Jo said. "You called Susan?"

"Yes. She's got your classes covered."

"Thank you."

"They're going to want to know when the funeral will be," she said gently.

Jo took a deep breath. "I guess tomorrow or Wednesday. There's no reason to wait longer. It's not like there are relatives to notify." She rolled away from Kelly, feeling tears coming again.

"Jo, I wish there was something I could do."

"You have. You've been here for me," she whispered.

"Don't push me away again," Kelly pleaded.

Jo turned back to her, reached up and touched her face. "I won't. I promise."

Kelly kissed her palm, then wiped her tears away.

Chapter Twenty-One

The whole day was a blur to Jo. Friends came and went. Betsy took off work and stayed with her. Jo called the same funeral home they had used when Beth died. The reality of Harry's death hit hard. She started crying, and Betsy took the phone from her and talked to the funeral director, finishing the arrangements. The funeral would be Wednesday.

"You've got to pick out a casket," Betsy said gently.

Jo nodded.

"Janis and I could do that for you, honey," Betsy offered.

"Would you really?" She knew she should have the strength to do this herself, but she just didn't.

"Yes. Don't worry about it, okay. We'll take care of it."

"I love you guys," she whispered.

Kelly came over at three, after her last class. She walked in, unmindful of the others there and took Jo in her arms.

"How are you holding up?" she said into her ear.

"Not too good," she admitted, though she felt better now that Kelly had arrived.

Kay came by after work, as did Deb, and Jo was touched. Everyone seemed to think that she would be in the mood to eat, as they all brought something.

"You need to eat something," Betsy insisted.

"I'm not really hungry," Jo said.

"Of course you're not, but you've got to eat." She went into the kitchen to make her a plate, and Jo looked wearily at Kelly.

"They're just trying to help," she said.

Jo nodded. "I know."

"Do you want everyone to leave?"

"I don't want you to leave," Jo said.

"No. I'm not leaving you," she whispered.

Jo forced down nearly half of what Betsy had piled on her plate and soon everyone was leaving.

"I'll come by tomorrow," Betsy said at the door.

"No. I'll be fine," Jo insisted.

"I'll be with her, Betsy," Kelly said.

"You will?" Jo asked, surprised. She had not expected her to miss school.

"I've cleared it with Susan."

When they were alone, Jo settled on the sofa and laid her head back.

"What can I get you?" Kelly asked.

"A drink," she said. "Strong."

"Coming right up."

Jo closed her eyes, thankful for the friends who had come today. They had meant well, even if it was exhausting for her. The only one she really wanted was Kelly, and she was here now, without question. Tomorrow would be difficult, probably more so than Wednesday. Tomorrow, she would say good-bye to Harry in private, at the lake.

"Here you go," Kelly said, handing her the drink.

"Thanks. And thanks for tomorrow, too."

Kelly looked at her with soft brown eyes, then took her hand and held it gently. "You've never told me about him."

Jo closed her eyes and laid her head back. "I never knew my father. He left before I was born," she said. "Though Harry was never a father. He spoiled me too much for that." She smiled.

"My mother was killed when I was twelve and I went to live with Harry and Beth. Whatever Beth said I couldn't do, Harry said I could."

"You've always called them by their first names?"

"Yes, as long as I can remember. Harry said it made him old before his time to call him grandfather. I think Beth preferred the more formal name, though I seldom called her that."

"What happened to your mother?" she asked.

"Car accident." Jo looked at her then. "She was an elementary school teacher."

"So you followed in her footsteps?"

"I think that's the main reason I became a teacher. I needed to connect to her, somehow. That seemed the only way. I hated it at first, though it sort of grew on me."

"You must be good," Kelly said.

Jo laughed. "I don't know. I sometimes think my classes are so very boring."

"Well, English. What do you expect?" Kelly teased.

Jo smiled at her and took her hand. "Thank you for being here."

"I want to take care of you," Kelly said softly.

Jo brought her hand up and kissed it. "Harry has been telling me for the last few months that I needed somebody. I told him that I was fine being alone." She shook her head. "But I was wrong."

"Do you want me to stay the night?" Kelly asked.

"What about your friend?"

"She left today."

Jo nodded. "Yes. I want you to stay with me. But only if you want to. Not because you feel you have to."

"I want to be with you. I like waking up with you," Kelly said softly.

Jo looked into her eyes and was frightened by what she saw there. Kelly didn't try to hide her feelings and Jo quickly looked away. She wasn't ready for that.

"I'm sorry," Kelly whispered. "Come here," and she pulled Jo into her arms.

Jo rested her head on Kelly's shoulder and closed her eyes. It would be so easy to love her, she thought. But she couldn't allow it. Not yet.

They went to bed a short time later. Jo closed her eyes, her hand curled around Kelly's breast, and felt safe. Kelly held her until she fell asleep.

Chapter Twenty-Two

They had a casserole for breakfast, one of the three that was in her refrigerator, and ate out on the deck, enjoying the warm November weather. It was another clear day, the sky blue and cloudless. They watched Bull Creek rush by as they ate in silence.

They had slept late, nearly until eight. Jo was still in Kelly's arms when the sun woke her, and she had watched for long moments while Kelly still slept. They had slept naked but they had not made love during the night, just like they had not the night before. As much as Jo wanted her, as much as she was attracted to her, she also just needed Kelly to be there for her. And Kelly was. Kelly seemed perfectly content to hold her during the night. Jo was convinced that what Kelly felt for her was more than just sexual attraction and it scared her. Maybe if they had made love, she could have believed it was all just physical, that Kelly was only hanging around for sex. But Kelly hadn't even tried. She had simply held Jo until she fell asleep and had still been holding her when she woke up. Jo didn't know which frightened her more.

"I think I want to take the boat out today, if that's okay," Jo said.

"Sure. Whatever you want."

"Harry loved the lake."

"Would you rather be alone out there, Jo?"

"No. I want you with me," she answered.

Kelly nodded and took their plates inside, leaving Jo alone with her thoughts.

By ten, Jo was pulling into Harry's driveway, where she parked in her usual spot and turned off the engine. Kelly said nothing as Jo stared at his house for a long moment before getting out.

They went inside, and Jo left Kelly in the living room while she went into Harry's bedroom to find his suit. As she walked in, she was overwhelmed with memories of him. His bed was still unmade. She swallowed back tears as she touched his pillow and smoothed the quilt that Beth had stitched. His dresser was cluttered with his personal things, his watch, change from his pockets, his keys. Her eyes flew around the room, picturing him there, going about his everyday business. She couldn't believe that he would never again walk in here, never again call her Jo-Jo.

She sat down on his bed and cried, her head in her hands. She should have seen him more. She should have been with him that morning.

Kelly heard her crying and walked into the room.

"Jo?"

"I should have been here. I could have helped him," she cried.

"Don't do this," Kelly said and sat down beside her. She put her arm around Jo and pulled her close. "You're not to blame, honey," she said gently. "He had a long, healthy life. He was happy out here, and now, as you said, he's gone to join his Beth."

"I know," she whispered. "You're right." She sat up and wiped her tears. "I'm sorry."

"You don't have to tell me you're sorry," Kelly said quietly.

"I'm okay now." Jo stood.

"Do you want me to find a suit?"

"No. I'll do it," she said and walked to his closet.

He only owned one suit. The one he had worn to Beth's funeral. It was only fitting that he should wear it to his own, as well. She opened his closet door and silently moved his clothes aside, finding the suit tucked back in the corner. She took it out, brushed the lint from it and hung it on the doorknob. She found his best dress shirt and then sorted through the few ties that he owned to find the dark red one, the one he had worn for Beth.

She stood staring into his closet for a long time, seeing the clothes that were so familiar to her. All his things, what was she going to do with them? She couldn't very well throw them out, as if they meant nothing to her. Then again, she couldn't let the house stay as it was, either. She suddenly realized that going through his house was going to be the hardest thing of all . . . so many memories.

Kelly gently touched her shoulder, bringing her back around. "Show me the boat."

Jo nodded. "Yeah. Let's go outside."

The boathouse was immaculate. All the gear put up just right, fishing rods hanging on the wall next to the ski equipment. As much as they liked to fish, they also enjoyed cruising the lake. So, the old bass boat had given way to a larger, more comfortable ski boat. It hung in the lift, out of the water. Jo walked over, turned the switch and watched it lower slowly into the lake. She didn't even remember putting it up the other night.

"Do you like the water?" Jo asked. It seemed important that she should.

Kelly nodded. "I love to swim. I just learned to ski last summer though," she added, with a wink. "I bet you're pretty good."

"I used to be. I only went a few times this summer. Mostly, we would go fishing or just cruising around."

"That's fun, too," Kelly said.

The boat bobbed gently on the water, and they climbed in. It started with one turn of the key as Harry had always kept the motor in excellent condition. Jo reversed the rudder and they slowly backed out of the slip. It was a warm day, but the wind was cool over the water. Kelly was silent, sitting opposite her in the front. Jo drove slowly around the lake, passing coves that she and Harry had fished in, boulders in the water where they had laid in the sun after swimming, and the cove with the fallen trees, a favorite bass spot. Jo pointed them all out to Kelly, who nodded and smiled at her. Jo was remembering Harry, saying good-bye to him and the times they had shared over the years.

They passed the mansions that had sprung up in the last ten years, and Jo told her how Harry had always complained about them.

"I like your grandfather's place better," Kelly said. "It's more of a home. These are just displays of wealth, trying to prove that you have more money than your neighbor."

"Yes, exactly."

"It's pretty out here," Kelly said later. "I've never been on Lake Travis on a boat."

"No? Where have you been?" she asked.

"Just Hippie Hollow," she grinned.

"Oh, yes. I remember," Jo said and nearly blushed. She remembered the time she had gone by it with Harry, looking for Kelly swimming nude.

Jo turned the boat around and headed back. It was very different being here without Harry, but she was glad Kelly was with her.

Back at the house, Jo went into the kitchen, thinking she should clean out Harry's refrigerator, but when she opened it and saw his things there, saw the food she had brought for their lunch that day, she just didn't have the heart. She shut it quickly.

Kelly was standing in the doorway, watching her. "All that can wait," she said gently.

"Yes. It'll have to be done, but I can't just yet."

"I'll help, when the time comes. So will Betsy and Janis."

Jo nodded and walked over to her. "You've been so nice to me these last few days. I don't know what I would have done without you."

Kelly reached for her, pulling her close. Jo moved into her arms and let herself be held.

"I'm ready to go now, I guess," she said quietly.

"Are you sure?"

"Yes. You probably have things you need to do today."

"No. I'm all yours," Kelly replied. "Unless you'd rather be alone?"

"I don't know." She pulled away. She was becoming too dependent on Kelly. She wanted to ask her to stay with her, to stay the night again, but she didn't. Maybe she did need to be alone, to have time to deal with his death.

Kelly seemed to read her thoughts. "We need to take his suit. You can call me later if you need anything," she offered.

Jo smiled her thanks and nodded.

Kelly took his suit into the funeral home while Jo waited in her car. She just couldn't go in. Kelly understood.

"Let me take it. I'll be right back."

Later, when they returned to Jo's house, Kelly took Jo in her arms and kissed her gently. Jo held her tightly, silently thanking her for all she had done.

"Please call if you need me," Kelly reminded her before leaving.

"I will," Jo promised, though she had no intention of calling. Tonight, she needed to be alone.

She let the answering machine pick up the five or six calls that came in. Most were from friends, checking on her. Others were from colleagues at school offering their sympathy. She appreciated their thoughts but was in no mood to talk to any of them. She took a beer, sat on her deck and stared at the creek as it rushed by. Two male cardinals sat at her feeder and fought over the few remaining seeds. She watched them and smiled.

Harry was gone, yet everything remained the same. The creek still flowed, the birds still scolded her for not keeping the feeder filled, the leaves fell like they did every year at this time. Life went on.

When it was too dark to see, she went in. Thinking of the food that her friends had brought she realized she was hungry and thankful for their kindness. She made a plate and stood by the microwave, watching the dish turn round and round as it heated. She poured a glass of wine, took her plate into the living room, sat in the silence and ate.

Later, she slowly turned the pages of a photo album, watching her life go by. She cried some, but not much. The photos were all taken at happy times in her life. There were many of Beth and Harry together, and she could see how much in love they were, even at the end. Harry had missed Beth terribly and now they were together again, she thought. Harry would be happy. As much as she had tried, she had never been able to replace Beth in his life. Jo knew she would miss him so very much, but she would be okay. Life went on.

She closed the book and was surprised at how much better she felt. Putting on some soft music, she poured another glass of wine, then went to the phone to call Betsy. She had left two messages, and Jo knew she was worried about her.

"I'm okay, really," Jo assured her.

"Is Kelly still there?"

"No. She left this afternoon."

"You know, if you need to come over, you can."

"I know, but I need to be alone. Thank you for worrying, though."

"What are friends for?"

"You're the best," Jo said.

"We'll see you tomorrow morning, then. Do you want us to pick you up?"

"No. I'll see you there," and hung up.

She thought about calling Kelly, but didn't. She didn't want to have the temptation of asking her to come over and sleep with her. That could too easily become a habit, she knew.

She finished her glass of wine, then got ready for bed. Reaching over to where Kelly had slept the last couple of nights, she gently rubbed the sheets. Kelly had come into her life so unexpectedly. Jo was afraid of the feelings that she had for Kelly. She wouldn't allow herself to fall in love with her, of course, but she did like her an awful lot. Where their relationship would go, she didn't know, but for now she just wanted to enjoy the time they had.

Chapter Twenty-Three

The funeral service was held in the small chapel in the funeral home. She couldn't remember a time Harry had ever been to church, other than Beth's funeral. As a child, Jo had gone every Sunday with her mother, but when she had moved in with her grandparents, only Beth had gone. She and Harry would sneak off for a morning of fishing or boat riding.

"We'll have our own church service out on the lake, Jo-Jo."

She smiled as she remembered him saying that on many a Sunday morning as Beth stood by and shook her head at them.

"It wouldn't hurt you a bit to go to church," she told him.

"Why press my luck?" Harry responded. "I wouldn't want Him to think that I was eager to join Him up there."

Various baskets and arrangements were a spot of cheeriness to an otherwise colorless day. She was surprised at the numerous flowers and plants that had been sent. Harry would find humor with that. He knew her luck with potted plants. Her eyes avoided the casket at the front and instead, she walked around, reading the cards from her friends. Susan and Arnie had sent a beautiful fall arrangement, and there were some from names she did not recognize. Harry's friends from the Senior Center, she supposed.

Before ten, people started arriving and she was surprised at how dressed up everyone was. Kelly walked in with Betsy and Janis, and Jo's eyes flew to hers.

Kelly smiled and walked up to her. Jo took in her dark gray suit with a colorful silk blouse underneath.

"Hi."

"Look at you. A skirt?" Jo teased.

"Yeah." Kelly shrugged. "I had to dig deep to find it."

"You look lovely," Jo said softly.

Kelly shrugged again and looked embarrassed, as most people do when they're not comfortable with what they're wearing. Jo doubted Kelly ever wore dresses.

"Hi, honey," Betsy said and hugged her. "You doing okay?"

Jo nodded. "The casket is beautiful," she said, although she had scarcely looked at it. She had decided on a closed casket. She didn't want her last memory of Harry to be lying in a casket. It was bad enough she pictured him so vividly in the hospital bed, so pale against the white sheets.

Betsy smiled and squeezed her shoulder, then went to sit down. Jo greeted the others as they came in, mostly her friends and a few of Harry's from the Senior Center. Of course, when you have no relatives and you're over 80, most of your old friends are already gone. She was surprised Kerry and Shea came. She didn't really know them that well. They were really Betsy and Janis's friends but she was touched that they had bothered. She told them as much. Kay was there, and she hugged Jo and kissed her cheek. Sharon and Mattie also came. Deb gave her a hug when she walked in and Jo thanked her. Susan and Arnie were there, too, and Jo wondered how many of the department's classes had been cancelled over the last few days.

Of the folks from the Senior Center, Jo knew only three. They were Harry's fishing buddies, whom she had seen at his house on several occasions. The others apparently had known him or had just come out of respect for one of their fallen members. She was glad when Mr. Daughtery, the youngest of the three at 75, asked her if he could speak at the service. She told him she thought Harry would have liked that.

The service was short, and when Mr. Daughtery stood up, he spoke for only a few minutes, telling them about Harry, his love of fishing and the lake, and especially his love for his "Jo-Jo." Fresh tears fell down Johanna's cheek, and Betsy put her arm around her and patted her shoulder. Jo smiled her thanks at Mr. Daughtery when he finished.

Nearly everyone walked to the cemetery, and it was only then, as they were lowering Harry into the ground, next to his beloved Beth, that Jo broke down and cried. Susan and Arnie were beside her. Arnie held her for a moment, offering his support.

Kelly walked up to her, gentle eyes looking into Jo's. Jo reached for her and held her tightly, needing her strength.

Afterward, they walked back together, and Jo thanked everyone for coming, accepting their hugs and sympathy with a smile. She had good friends.

She walked with Kelly to her Explorer, thanking her again for all she had done. "We've got our last softball game tonight. It's an early game. I thought you might want to get out of the house," she suggested.

"Yes. I think I might. I don't really want to spend the evening alone."

"Good. We were going to go out afterwards and get a burger or something. Maybe you'll be hungry by then."

"Okay."

"I've got to get to class," she said. "I'll pick you up about five."

Betsy and Janis were the only ones still there. Betsy insisted that Jo come home with them.

"No. I'll be fine."

"You don't need to be alone, honey," Janis said.

"Actually, I was thinking that a nap sounded pretty good. I'm going with Kelly to the game tonight, by the way."

"You are? Are you sure?" Betsy asked.

"Yes. I'd like to be around my friends tonight, I think."

"Okay. You sure you don't want to come home with us?"

"Thank you, but no. You two have both done so much for me this week," she said as she hugged them both.

On the way home, she was surprised at how good she felt. It was over with, this formality. She had said good-bye to Harry yesterday and last night, and now he was at rest.

She took time for lunch, heating more casserole. She threw out what was left, planning to wash the dishes and return them at the game tonight. Afterward, she sat on her deck with her plate and her iced tea. The birdseed was all gone and before she started eating, she refilled the feeder. Soon the male cardinals were back, and she watched them while she ate.

Later, she laid down, not really sleepy, just tired. She was surprised when she woke up at four. She showered, got dressed and sat down to wait for Kelly. It was so quiet. She realized she was thinking of everything except Harry. That wasn't necessarily good, but at this point, she was just looking forward to going out and being around people, where the conversation wasn't on death.

Kelly knocked on her door at exactly five o'clock. Standing there in her softball uniform, she smiled at Jo.

"You look better," she said, when Jo opened the door.

"Did I look bad before?"

"You looked tired."

"I took a nap today," Jo smiled.

Kelly nodded and smiled warmly back. "Ready?"

Jo nodded and locked the door behind her.

On the way to South Austin, Kelly reached over and took her hand. "I'm glad you're going tonight."

Jo's fingers entwined with hers. "Me, too."

The fields were not yet crowded, as it was the first game. Kelly took a small cooler from the back. "I brought you a lawn chair. And I packed you a couple of beers. I thought you might want one."

"Thanks. I think I will," she said quietly.

"Jo? Are you okay?"

Jo nodded and smiled. "Yes," she said, a little too brightly. She was suddenly very tired.

"Maybe this wasn't a good idea. I just thought that you should get out."

"I'll be fine. Don't worry about me."

"I can't help but worry about you," she said and met Jo's eyes. "I. . . ."

"I'm fine, really," Jo said, cutting her off. The look in Kelly's eyes scared her, as it always did.

Kelly nodded, and they walked to the field. Betsy and Janis were already there, and Jo put the lawn chair next to them as Kelly left to warm up.

She took a beer from the cooler and sat down, smiling at Betsy and Janis. They both had concerned looks on their faces, and she smiled again.

"Really, I'm ok" she said. And she was. Her emotions felt a little raw, that's all.

"I'm glad you came," Betsy said. "You don't need to sit home by yourself."

"Where are we going for dinner?" she asked.

"I think Gordie's Sports Pub," Janis said. "At least, that's what Deb said."

Jo nodded and her glance found Kelly as she was throwing with Kay. She had missed watching her play softball. She was so confident, so strong. Jo watched her and smiled.

"How are you two getting along?" Betsy asked, following her gaze.

Jo looked away quickly. "Okay."

When the team took the field, Jo's eyes followed Kelly to third base, watching as Kelly smoothed the dirt with her foot, a ritual that never failed to amuse Jo. Her eyes followed Kelly's every movement, and she saw Kelly watching her. Jo silently scolded Kelly for not paying attention to the game, but when a ball was hit sharply to third, Kelly grabbed it easily and threw a strike to first. Jo clapped, and Kelly grinned at her.

Kelly hit two home runs, both to deep center field and Jo stood and cheered as she rounded third, stepping on home plate for the second time. Kelly met her eyes and winked as she passed by, and Jo grinned back.

The only damper on Jo's evening was when Lucy showed up. She sat on the other side of Kerry and Shea. Jo glanced at her several times, knowing that Lucy's eyes were glued on Kelly. She felt a stab of jealousy but ignored it.

Lucy was nothing to Kelly, nor had she been. She believed Kelly had told her the truth.

They finished the season undefeated and Jo joined the others behind the dugout after the game. Deb came up to her immediately and asked how she was doing.

"Okay," she said and smiled.

"Are you going to dinner with us?" she asked.

"Yes, I think it'll be fun."

"Listen, do you want to ride with me? I'll bring you back for your car afterward," Deb said.

"Oh, no. I came with Kelly," Jo told her.

"Oh. Is she still hanging around?"

"Yes."

"Well, I guess what with your grandfather and all...."

Jo refused to acknowledge her remark. She and Deb had been friends for years. She didn't think that Deb actually meant what she said.

"Thank you for the flowers, by the way. They were lovely," she said.

"If you need me for anything, Jo, I'll be there," Deb offered.

"Thank you. That's very kind," she replied, but her eyes were drawn to Lucy, who had walked up to talk to Kelly. Jo watched them intently, her eyes moving from one to the other, but she saw no sign of any intimacy between them and was relieved.

Deb followed her gaze. “She dropped her like a hot potato, I guess.” She turned to Jo. “What do you see in her? My God, she’s slept with half the softball team!”

“Stop it!” Jo snapped. Then her voice softened. “Deb, my relationship with Kelly is my business,” she said, tapping her chest. “I appreciate your concern, but I’m a big girl. I can take care of myself.”

"You're making a mistake, Jo."

"Perhaps."

Deb shrugged. "When she's through with you, give me a call. I'll still be around."

Jo refused to get angry, and she let Deb have the last word. Walking away, Jo realized the distance between her and Deb was nearly insurmountable.

Kelly was waiting for her, and Jo pushed thoughts of Deb aside, greeting Kelly with a smile.

"You had a wonderful game, as always," Jo told Kelly as they walked to the Explorer.

"As always?"

"Well, every game I've seen," Jo said.

"Maybe you should come to all of them, then. I seem to play better when you're around."

"Were you showing off?" Jo asked with a smile.

Kelly shrugged. "Maybe."

She drove over to the restrooms, where most of the others had gone, to change out of her uniform. Jo waited and soon she came back wearing faded jeans and a sweater.

"Better?"

"Yeah. Though a shower would have been wonderful," Kelly said.

They drove down Riverside to Gordie's Sports Pub, famous for its half-pound burgers served on giant buns baked on the spot. Kelly parked and turned off the engine, but before she could get out, Jo stopped her.

"Can I ask you something?"

"Of course," Kelly said.

"It's about Lucy," she said.

"Oh. I saw you talking to Deb earlier. What did she say this time?" she asked.

"Nothing about Lucy, really. She said the only reason you were still around was because of Harry."

"God, Jo, you don't believe that?" she asked softly.

Jo met her eyes. "No." She looked away. "When you said that you and Lucy had gone out, what does that mean, exactly?" she asked.

"Jo . . ." Kelly gripped the steering wheel and let out a heavy sigh.

"I'm not trying to pick a fight with you, Kelly. I just need to know. You obviously had some sort of relationship with her."

"When I first moved here, we went out a couple of times. I guess you'd call it a date. But the last month or so, whenever we went out, it was as friends. On my part, at least. Movies, dinner, things like that. I haven't been out dancing with her, if that's what you mean."

"And when you kissed her, was it on the cheek?"

"No."

Of course, Jo knew that it wasn't, but she was filled with such jealousy that it scared her.

Kelly took her hand and made Jo look at her. "Do you remember that first time we kissed? While we were dancing?"

Jo nodded.

"Now that was a kiss," she said softly. "It nearly brought me to my knees." Kelly looked away and released Jo's hand. "You didn't want me. Lucy did. But when I kissed her I felt nothing. Absolutely nothing."

Jo stared at her profile, knowing she was hiding the hurt in her eyes for all the times Jo had sent her away.

"I'm sorry you thought I didn't want you," she whispered.

Kelly turned back to her and looked into her eyes. "Did you?"

Jo nodded and she wanted very badly to kiss her now. "I won't bring up Lucy again. I just wanted to know how involved you were with her."

"You're the only one that I've wanted, Jo."

They stared at each other for a long moment, then Kelly looked away. "We better go in," she said.

Jo nodded and got out, closing the door just as Deb drove up with Lucy. She silently cringed and managed a smile as the two of them got out. Lucy glared at Jo, who suddenly felt like the "other" woman, and she hated it. She watched as Lucy's glance slid to Kelly, and Jo could see the hurt in her eyes.

"Hey, you two," Deb greeted them, and Jo could tell how forced it was.

Kelly grabbed Jo's arm, stopping her. "I forgot my money. I'll catch up."

She was gone before Jo could stop her. She had enough money for both of them.

Jo didn't miss the irony of her situation, and she smiled apologetically at Deb and Lucy, as they all continued walking.

"Well, congratulations," Lucy said sarcastically. "I guess you've won."

Jo bristled. "I didn't realize there was a contest."

Lucy's laugh was bitter. "She'll fuck you over just like she does everyone."

Jo refused to be baited.

"But she's good, huh?" Lucy continued.

"How would you know?" Jo asked.

For a second, Jo thought she was about to be slapped, but Deb pulled Lucy away.

"Let's go inside," Deb suggested, but Lucy jerked her arm away.

"I love her," Lucy spat.

Oh, she's so young, Jo thought. "I'm sorry." She didn't know what else to say.

"Fuck you."

Lucy hurried inside and Jo wondered how such animosity could be between them when they hardly knew each other. It wasn't fair.

She turned to Deb. "I'm sorry."

"She's just hurt."

"I know," Jo nodded. "I've been there." She motioned to the door. "Go ahead. I'll wait for Kelly here."

But Kelly was already walking up.

"What happened?"

Jo shook her head. "Nothing."

"Jo?"

She tried to laugh. "Lucy's in love with you."

"I've done nothing to make her believe there could ever be anything between us," Kelly insisted. "Please believe me."

"I do. She's just hurting."

"And she took it out on you?"

Jo nodded, then cupped Kelly's face. "Better me than you. You're the one she's in love with."

Their eyes locked for an instant, and Jo wondered if Kelly's relationship with Lucy would forever haunt her.

"Come on."

The others were already there, but Betsy and Janis had saved them seats and Jo was thankful. She had no desire to sit anywhere near Lucy and Deb for fear of a repeat of the scene in the parking lot. They ordered several pitchers of beer and passed them around the table, everyone filling her own glass. Gordie's was where most of the softball teams came after games, and the crowd, as usual, was informal and rowdy. They had an outdoor patio and sand pits for volleyball during the summer. Tonight, the patio was closed, and inside it was crowded and loud.

Jo ordered one of the big burgers, though she knew she would never eat it all. She never did. She did her best to ignore the two pairs of eyes across the table from them. She hated to think that her friendship with Deb was threatened, but she could never feel anything romantic for Deb. There just wasn't a spark there for her. She wished Deb could see that.

Kelly leaned closer to her so she could talk to Betsy and Janis, and their thighs touched often. Jo was very aware of her. Whenever she met Kelly's eyes, she could see that Kelly felt the same. Whatever this was between them, their attraction for each other had not dimmed. If anything, it was stronger than ever. Jo had to force herself not to reach out and touch her.

By the time their burgers were served, Jo's appetite for food had vanished. She had to force down what little she ate, although Kelly seemed to have no problem with her appetite.

"Aren't you hungry?" she asked.

"Not for food, no."

Their eyes met for a brief second, and Jo was certain that everyone at the table could tell what she was thinking. She looked away quickly and picked up the giant burger, taking a large bite.

The meal seemed to last for hours, and Jo pretended to be interested in the conversations going on around her, when all she wanted was to go home and take Kelly with her. Finally, the table was cleared and the leftovers boxed as they passed around the last pitcher of beer.

Betsy nudged her. "You've been awfully quiet."

"Not really."

"Are you okay?" She looked at her. "Deb and Lucy have been shooting you two daggers all evening. What gives?"

"It's very simple. Lucy wants Kelly. Deb wants me," Jo admitted.

"I see," Betsy said with raised eyebrows. "And who do you want?"

"Betsy!"

Betsy laughed, and Janis demanded to know what was so funny.

At last, they got up to go. Everyone said their good-byes, as some of them would not see each other until the next season started in the spring.

Jo and Kelly walked out with Betsy and Janis, who couldn't keep from smiling. Jo didn't care anymore. All she wanted was to be alone with Kelly.

"I'll call you tomorrow. You'll be at work?" Betsy asked.

"Yes."

"I guess I shouldn't worry that you'll be alone tonight."

"I'll be fine, Betsy," Jo assured her with a smile.

Once in the Explorer, with seatbelts safely fastened, they allowed themselves to touch freely. Kelly took Jo's hand and placed it on her thigh, and Jo felt the muscles in her leg contract as Kelly drove. Her thigh was warm to the touch. Jo let her hand rub gently to Kelly's knee, then back up. Kelly glanced at her, then covered her hand with her own, preventing any further exploration.

They didn't speak on the drive home, and Kelly drove quickly, speeding up MoPac, ignoring the speed limit. Jo didn't mind.

Kelly pulled into Jo's drive and cut the engine. They sat in silence as they looked at each other.

"Do you want me to go?" Kelly finally asked.

"No. I want you to stay," Jo said softly.

Kelly took her hand and brought it to her lips. "Do you know how much I want you?"

"Hopefully, as much as I want you."

They made it just inside the front door before their desire could wait no more. Kelly held her, fiercely pushing her up against the closed door, pressing against her as her lips sought Jo's. Jo's mouth opened for her kiss, and her tongue met Kelly's. Her hands shoved Kelly's sweater up and touched warm skin, moving quickly to her breasts.

"God, you feel so good," Jo breathed into her mouth.

Kelly drew back and pushed Jo away. "Wait," she said, her breath coming quickly. "I've got to shower."

"No. Later," Jo insisted, reaching for her again, this time her hands going to Kelly's jeans.

Their kisses were wet and hard. Jo turned Kelly quickly, pinning her back against the door, and shoving her thigh between Kelly's legs.

"I just want to be inside you," Jo breathed, and her fingers fumbled with Kelly's as they struggled to get her jeans off.

Jo's impatient hands could wait no more, and she pushed past silk, groaning loudly when her fingers found the heat between Kelly's thighs.

Her mouth went back to Kelly's, her tongue plunging inside, her thigh holding Kelly to the door as her fingers drove deep inside her.

"Oh, Christ!" Kelly hands clutched Jo's shoulders, and her hips thrust up, matching Jo's rhythm. "Don't stop," she begged.

"I won't stop. I want you so badly."

Jo's fingers were coated with Kelly's wetness. She thrust into her again and again as Kelly's ragged breathing echoed in her ears.

Jo's arm ached as Kelly neared her orgasm, but she didn't stop until Kelly screamed her pleasure, once, twice, and a third time before her hips stilled.

Her weight settled on Jo, and Jo held her against the door until their breathing slowed.

"I guess I didn't really need a shower," Kelly finally managed.

"Oh, yes. I think you need a shower," Jo smiled wickedly. "I think we both do."

They hurried down the hall to the bathroom, shedding clothes as they went. The hot spray hit Jo's shoulders, but it was not nearly as hot as the mouth at her breast. Kelly's hands cupped her hips, bringing Jo flush against her, and Jo tipped her head back, offering her breasts to Kelly, feeling nearly drunk with desire.

Kelly's mouth was wet when it captured Jo's. Streams of water washed over their faces as Jo's hands slid up Kelly's wet arms, circling her back. Soapy hands touched her, moving over her breasts, down to her stomach and hips. When those same slippery hands slid between her legs, Jo felt weak, and she anchored herself to Kelly, their moans mingling as Kelly's fingers slipped inside her.

"That feels so good," Jo murmured.

She felt Kelly tremble in her arms, and Kelly's fingers left her.

"I want my mouth on you," she whispered into Jo's ear.

Kelly knelt in front of her. Jo looked down at her, their eyes holding for a long moment. Then Jo's slid shut, and she leaned against the slick tile as her hands guided Kelly to her.

Jo's breath left her at the first touch of Kelly's tongue, and when Kelly's arms slid around her hips, pulling Jo more firmly against her mouth, she cried out. Her hands pressed against the shower walls as hot water cascaded over her back.

Her legs felt weak and shaky, and she leaned into Kelly, her eyes still closed, lost in Kelly's desire for her. Kelly's mouth devoured her, and Jo felt every stroke of her tongue.

With warm water flowing over her body, she felt the first waves of ecstasy. She pushed herself against Kelly's hot mouth. Her breath caught, and she clutched Kelly's head, holding Kelly to her as wave after wave crashed through her, finally uttering the scream she had been holding back.

Jo had never wanted someone like this before. She had never needed someone as much as she did Kelly at this moment.

With shaking hands, she toweled herself off. When she was finished, she looked up. Kelly stood in the bathroom doorway, watching her, the light behind her outlining her glistening body.

"Come to bed." Kelly's words were barely a whisper across the room.

Kelly laid down and pulled Jo to her, kissing her mouth with such urgency that it frightened her. Their tongues dueled, and Jo pushed Kelly back, settling her weight on top of her.

"I want you so much," Jo whispered. Her hands cupped Kelly's face, and she kissed her gently. Kelly lay still, letting Jo set the pace. Her earlier need to hurry had vanished. Instead, she wanted to savor every kiss, every touch. She slowly forced her mouth from Kelly's, lips gliding over Kelly's eyes and cheeks, over her ears and neck. Kelly's hands gently caressed her back, moving to her shoulders and back down again.

"Do you have any idea what you do to me?" Kelly whispered. She brought her hands to Jo's face and guided her mouth back to hers. "No one has ever made me feel the way you do. Jo, you must know I'm. . ."

Jo silenced her with a kiss. She didn't want to hear the words she feared Kelly wanted to say.

"Shhh," she breathed into her mouth.

Her hands caressed Kelly's breasts, then she put her mouth there and her tongue licked at Kelly's nipple, teasing the hard peak, then sucking it hungrily into her mouth.

"Oh," Kelly sighed and her hands held Jo there for a long moment.

Jo moved her mouth to Kelly's other breast, and her hand slid slowly down Kelly's smooth body, finding her wet with need. For me, Jo thought. Her fingers slid into Kelly's wetness, and Kelly's legs parted and her hips rose up. Jo's fingers stilled and she pressed into Kelly as her mouth continued its assault on her breast.

Finally, she drew her mouth away and found Kelly's lips again, meeting her tongue, sliding into her mouth. She couldn't get enough of her, and her hand left Kelly's warmth and cupped her face again as they kissed.

Jo drew back and looked into Kelly's eyes, emotions swelling up inside of her. She pushed away the feelings that threatened her so. She couldn't allow them in.

Shutting her eyes for a brief moment, she moved down Kelly's body, her tongue hinting at what lay ahead. Kelly pushed at her shoulders, silently begging her to hurry.

Jo lay between Kelly's legs and pushed them apart with her hands. Her tongue teased Kelly's inner thighs, and Kelly let her breath out slowly.

"Take me, please," she pleaded.

And Jo did. Her mouth settled over Kelly, and her tongue moved into her wetness, stroking her quickly.

"God, yes," Kelly breathed.

Jo wrapped her arms around Kelly's hips, and she pressed closer to her, her tongue swirling over her, into her, as Kelly surged up under her mouth. Jo's lips caressed her quickly and then slowed. She wasn't nearly ready for this to end, and Kelly gripped her shoulders hard, pushing her down.

"You're driving me crazy," Kelly gasped.

Jo knew that she was and she savored the control, her tongue stroking Kelly slowly, tasting her sweetness, tormenting Kelly to an even higher peak. She would never tire of this, Jo thought, and her lips again settled over Kelly, sucking her into her mouth, causing Kelly to groan loudly.

"Please," Kelly begged, and Jo gave way to her pleadings as her tongue moved quickly over Kelly, bringing her to the brink of orgasm and then over the edge, not stopping until Kelly cried out with her release.

Kelly pressed Jo's mouth to her, her hands holding her hair, her hips rising and meeting her, her body shuddering, until she slowly laid back down, her arms limp by her sides.

Jo drew away, then came back and kissed her there gently, then laid down beside her, one leg stretched over her.

"I can't move," Kelly groaned.

Jo smiled and caressed her face, her closed eyes, her swollen lips.

They lay on their sides, facing each other, the words whisper-soft between them.

"Each time with you is more than the time before," Kelly murmured. "I didn't think it was possible."

Jo said nothing, just looked at her, touched her. She was afraid to speak, afraid of what she was feeling.

Kelly opened her eyes and looked at Jo.

"What is it? What are you thinking?"

Jo shook her head slowly, entwining her legs with Kelly's. Her hands wouldn't leave Kelly's warm skin. They moved over Kelly's stomach, her breasts, her neck, Jo's eyes following her hands every movement, as if they had a will of their own.

"Does it frighten you, what I feel for you?" Kelly whispered.

"Don't."

Jo closed her eyes tightly, and her hands stilled.

"Not saying it doesn't make it any less true," Kelly said gently.

"I'm not ready for that," Jo admitted.

Kelly sighed wearily, and Jo found her eyes, catching just a glimpse of hurt there. She didn't know what to say.

"I'm sorry, Jo."

Jo shook her head slowly. "There's nothing for you to be sorry for. It's me," she said, tapping her chest lightly.

Kelly pushed Jo down on the bed and moved up beside her, touching her face lightly with her fingertips.

"You're such a beautiful lover. I hope I bring you as much pleasure as you do me," Kelly murmured into her ear.

"Like no one ever has before," Jo said and held her. "It scares me."

Kelly smiled in the darkness and touched her lips lightly. "I won't hurt you," she whispered so quietly that Jo wasn't sure she heard the words. "I just want to love you."

Jo closed her eyes and let out a soft sigh as Kelly began to do just that. Her mouth nuzzled Jo's neck and her hand cupped her breast, her thumb raking over Jo's nipple. Jo thrilled in the feel of Kelly's mouth and lips on her, and she relaxed, letting the lovemaking take over her senses. Her nipples were taut and ready for Kelly's touch, and Kelly's tongue caressed them lightly before her mouth covered each peak in turn. Jo brushed her fingers through Kelly's hair and down her back, her breath coming quickly.

Kelly lay on top of her, shoving her leg between Jo's thighs. Jo arched into it, wrapping one leg around her. Kelly again moved to her mouth and kissed her with such sweetness that Jo thought she would cry. Her hands cupped Kelly's face and she held her mouth to her, their lips brushing lightly against each other. Oh, she could get so used to this, this slow, sweet lovemaking.

Kelly leaned on her elbow, her hand cradling Jo's head. "You're so beautiful," she whispered into her ear. Her hand moved down Jo's body, caressing her. Her leg pressed hard against Jo, and Jo opened up further, rising to meet her. Her mouth settled over Jo's breast again and her fingers slid between her own leg and Jo's body. She touched her, so wet and ready, and Kelly slid her fingers into her, deep inside her, and Jo cried out and held her close.

But Kelly pulled away.

"Roll over," she said urgently.

Jo turned onto her stomach, trembling. Then Kelly's warm body covered her, hands and mouth tempting, teasing.

With Jo's face buried in the pillow, she closed her eyes, arms stretched out in front of her, thrilling to the pleasure of Kelly's touch.

She felt her breathing quicken as Kelly's hands moved over her hips, dipping between her thighs, then back out again. Her hips rose off the bed when Kelly's hands lightly brushed the backs of her thighs, and her legs parted instinctively.

Kelly slipped one hand under her, lifting her. Jo's breathing was labored now as she waited for Kelly to come to her.

She felt Kelly's other hand move between her thighs, and she moaned loudly, anticipating her touch. Then Kelly's fingers were there, first two, then three, and she plunged into her, hard.

Jo's hips jerked again, but Kelly held her, one hand moving under her, stroking her, as her other hand glided in and out of her wetness. Jo's fists clutched at the bed sheet, her hips writhing as she tried to match Kelly's rhythm.

But it was too much. Jo was gasping now, being carried away, and Kelly's fingers moved faster still, harder. She couldn't take it another second, and Jo's body exploded.

Behind her closed lids, she saw stars, and she screamed out, a loud, primitive scream, her clenched fists pulling the bed sheet lose as her body collapsed on the bed.

Kelly lay down beside her, her fingers still inside. She moved them once and Jo groaned.

"I can't move," Jo said hoarsely. "Don't you dare."

She heard Kelly's low chuckle as she slowly pulled her fingers away, and Jo managed to turn onto her side.

"I see I've rendered you speechless," Kelly teased.

"You've rendered me useless."

Kelly laughed and kissed Jo hard on the mouth.

"I don't think so," Kelly whispered.

Her hand lightly nudged Jo's shoulder, pushing her onto her back. Jo's eyes were closed, her breathing still ragged as Kelly slid slowly down her body, her mouth kissing her urgently as she moved. Jo's legs were still limp on the bed. She knew she didn't have the energy to respond. But still, she wanted to feel Kelly's mouth on her, her tongue on her, inside of her. She couldn't wait any longer. She placed her hands on Kelly's shoulders and guided her between her legs.

"Please, I need you so much," she begged.

Her legs opened wide as Kelly settled between them and Jo gasped when Kelly's mouth covered her. She felt Kelly's tongue slide over her, and she was lost. She lay back, her hands gripping the sheets, pulling at them as she felt Kelly's tongue plunge inside of her.

"Oh, dear God," she breathed. Her body was spent, should be spent, but still it opened to Kelly, responded to her lovemaking. She closed her eyes tightly, letting her mind go blank, thinking of nothing except this woman and her mouth on her.

Kelly stroked her, her mouth devouring her, and Jo thought she would surely die from pleasure. Her hips arched and her heels dug into the bed as the first wave of orgasm hit her. She cried out, then groaned softly as her body exploded under Kelly's mouth.

Jo pulled Kelly close to her and held her tightly as she felt tears well in her eyes. Kelly made love to her in such a way that left no doubt of her feelings. Jo stubbornly denied the feelings that were gripping at her own heart. She didn't want this woman to love her. She wanted their relationship to remain as it was: physical, sexual, but not emotional. She couldn't handle that. She would not let Kelly into her heart. She could not.

They didn't speak, and Jo was thankful. Kelly didn't mention her tears, she simply kissed them away and held Jo beside her, brushing her hair softly until Jo fell asleep in her arms.

Chapter Twenty-Four

Jo walked into her office and stared at the stacks of papers littering her desk. It would take days to get it cleaned off. Morning classes had been a chore and she wondered if maybe she had come back too soon. Susan had told her to take the entire week off, but she didn't know what she would do with herself, alone. She wanted to get back into the routine of her life and put the last week behind her.

Kelly had left early that morning to go to her apartment to shower and dress. They did not speak about the night before and she knew what Kelly was thinking, that Jo was going to send her away again. Jo could see it in her eyes, and she hated herself for it. She had kissed Kelly and held her and told her everything was fine. It was, really. She wouldn't stop seeing Kelly. She couldn't deny herself that. It was just too much, too soon, was all.

She was busy sorting papers on her desk when Kelly walked in later. She glanced at the clock, surprised that it was after one. Kelly held a sack up and smiled.

"Tuna on wheat, extra mustard," she said and laid the bag on top of the papers Jo was recording. "You need to eat."

Jo smiled at her. "What makes you think I haven't already had lunch?"

"You never have lunch unless I make you," she said. "I gotta run."

She turned back at the door. "Don't forget to eat it, now."

"Thank you. I won't."

Kelly left, and Jo munched on the sandwich while she worked. She was hungry. She hadn't taken time for breakfast, and Kelly was right. She rarely ate lunch.

It was a very long day, and Jo had to force herself to keep her last class until the scheduled time. She wrapped things up with ten minutes to spare and told them to have a nice afternoon, then hurried to her office. The mounds of papers on her desk were haunting her, and she stayed until nearly six, trying to put her office in order.

Kelly had not come by. Jo found her office closed and locked. She should be thankful. She needed time alone. After the night they had spent together, she needed some time to separate herself from Kelly. Her emotions felt all tangled, as they always did when she spent a night in Kelly's arms. She was having a hard enough time just getting through the day with bits and pieces of their night together flashing in front of her, and at the most awkward times, too. But once at home, she was restless. She opened her refrigerator, searching for something for dinner. There was nothing. She opened her pantry, grimacing at the two cans of soup that confronted her.

"Yuck," she said, closing the door. She needed to go shopping, she realized. She stood in the kitchen, indecisive. Just last week, she would have been able to call Harry and go to his place for dinner. She closed her eyes and stopped her thoughts right there. It would do her no good to think about that.

She could always call Betsy and Janis and see what they were doing for dinner, maybe invite herself over. She'd done it before. She knew she was deliberately omitting Kelly from her choices. She could call her. She knew that Kelly would meet her anywhere for dinner. But then, afterward, she would ask if Jo wanted her to come home with her, and Jo didn't want to be in that situation. She knew if she was, she would ask Kelly to stay again and they couldn't keep doing that. She needed some time away from Kelly, away from the feelings Kelly stirred in her heart.

She walked over to the phone and punched out Betsy's number.

"Jo! We were just talking about you," Janis said.

"I hope it was good," she smiled.

"How are you?" Janis asked.

"Hungry. What are you doing for dinner?"

Janis laughed. "We were just arguing over who was going to cook and Betsy decided on ordering pizza. Do you want to come over?"

"Yes, I'd love to. Sure you don't mind?"

"Don't be silly. Come over."

Twenty minutes later, Jo was knocking on their door. Betsy opened it and greeted her with a hug.

"How was it today?"

"Long," Jo said. "But okay."

"Good. Come on in."

"Hi, Jo," Janis called from the kitchen. She brought out a beer for Johanna. "Where's Kelly?"

"I don't know," Jo said.

"Is everything okay?" Betsy asked.

"I guess."

"I thought last night that you two. . . I mean, you looked like. . . Oh, hell, you know what I mean," she finished weakly.

Jo smiled. "Yes. I know what you mean. I saw her at lunch, but we didn't really get a chance to talk. I haven't seen her since."

"She didn't stay with you last night?"

Jo blushed and looked away. "Yes," she said quietly. "She stayed with me."

"But?"

"But, nothing."

"Oh, Jo, I know you better than that. What's wrong?"

"Betsy, I don't know," she admitted. "I like her a lot. I'm just scared, I guess."

"She's not Nancy," Betsy stated.

"I know. But I'm just not ready for a relationship right now."

"You must know how it is with her," Janis said.

Jo looked at her and nodded. "Yes, I know."

"She told you?"

Jo shook her head. "She doesn't need to tell me," she said quietly.

Jo thought back to last night and the way that they had made love. No, Kelly didn't need to say the words. She had tried, but Jo had stopped her.

"I wish you would give her a chance," Betsy said.

"I just can't. I can’t go through that again, Betsy."

"So you spend the rest of your life alone, just so you don't take a chance on getting hurt? Jo, nothing's guaranteed. Not for any of us. Who's to say that one day Janis won't meet someone who sweeps her off her feet and she up and leaves me?"

"Me?" Janis protested.

"Well, I know there's no one else out there for me," Betsy said and smiled lovingly at her.

Janis smiled at her. "Thanks," she said softly.

Jo watched them and was jealous. She wanted what they had and she realized suddenly that she had never had that with Nancy. She thought they had been happy together, but really, had they ever had the close intimacy that Betsy and Janis seemed to share? They had lived two separate lives. They had their own friends and they rarely mixed the two. Jo had frequently gone out with Betsy and Janis without Nancy, and Nancy had seldom included Jo when she was out with her friends. How strange it all seemed now. Most of Nancy's friends were from the corporate world, from where she worked. Jo didn't have much in common with them and was secretly pleased that she didn't have to endure too many outings with them. Of course, Nancy had met someone from that world, someone who she had much more in common with than Johanna. And it was easy for her to leave, it seemed. She showed no remorse when she packed her things and moved to New York. Jo was the one left broken. It wasn't so much that Nancy had left her, she realized now. It was that she had felt cheated all those years. It was like they had lived a lie for a long time, and she was saddened to think that if Nancy had not left her, they would still be living together, pretending their relationship was perfect. It saddened her also to think that she would not have met Kelly.

"What I'm trying to say," Betsy started, but Jo cut her off.

"I know what you're trying to say," Jo said. "I just have to work this out in my own way, in my own time."

Betsy nodded. "Okay. Enough of that."

The doorbell rang, and Jo was spared. Pizza had arrived.

Chapter Twenty-Five

Jo had missed Kelly terribly the night before, and she missed her again at lunch today. She looked for her at twelve-thirty and again at one, but she never came. Jo finally picked up the phone and called her office, but she wasn't in. Her last class was out at noon on Fridays, and Jo assumed she had gone home. She wondered why Kelly was avoiding her.

She hung up, pushed Kelly from her mind and went to work sorting the papers her assistant had graded for her. After her last class at three, she went to her office, then decided against staying and locked up. It was Friday. Most everyone else had already gone for the weekend.

She met Susan in the hall as she was leaving.

"Johanna. I've been meaning to come see you the last

two days, but I've had meetings scheduled nonstop, it seems. How are you holding up?"

"I'm doing okay, Susan. Thanks. Thanks for all you've done."

"Arnie and I were wondering what you were planning for Thanksgiving?" she asked.

"I hadn't really thought about it," she admitted. Jo had always spent the holidays with Harry and Beth, then later, with only Harry. He cooked enough for eight or ten people, even when it was only the two of them. They then would spend the next week eating turkey and wouldn't crave it again until the next year. Last year, he had invited Betsy and Janis, and after stuffing themselves, they had sat around watching football the rest of the day.

"Well, we would love for you to join us. David and Sarah will both be here this year," she said, referring to their two grown children.

"I appreciate the offer, Susan. I'll let you know," she replied, but she knew she wouldn't go. If she did anything for Thanksgiving, she would spend it with Betsy and Janis. Or Kelly, she added.

"Well, think about it. I know you have friends here that will probably invite you, too, but we would love for you to spend it with our family."

"Thank you. And thank Arnie for me, too."

She drove home slowly, not in a hurry to rush the weekend. She would have to go to Harry's house tomorrow and start cleaning and sorting through his things. The reminder of Thanksgiving brought on a rush of sadness. It would be hard not having Harry with her through the holidays this year. Especially Christmas, she thought.

Her house was quiet and empty. She changed into sweatpants and cursed herself for not going grocery shopping. She had two beers in the refrigerator. She opened one and sat in the living room, watching a light rain fall on the deck. Winter was showing itself this evening, and they were expecting their first frost of the season. She looked at her potted plants dripping in the cold rain and got up to bring them inside. These three were the only ones still alive after the hot summer. It was probably best that Arnie had not given her any more plants.

She sat back on the sofa, grabbed the remote and flipped through the channels, finding nothing to interest her. She switched off the TV and sighed. Why hadn't Kelly called her? Why hadn't she come by to see her? Was she waiting for Jo to call her?

Johanna looked at the phone for a moment, then picked it up and punched out her number.

Kelly answered on the second ring.

"What are you doing?" Jo asked.

"Just sitting here," she replied.

"Me, too."

Kelly said nothing, so Jo continued. "I missed you today," she confessed.

"I missed you, too."

"Would you like to have dinner . . . or something?" Jo asked.

There was silence for a moment and Jo pictured her smiling over the "or something."

"I could pick up Chinese and come over, if you'd like," Kelly offered.

"I'd like that."

"Good. What kind do you want?"

"Anything with chicken. And an eggroll."

"Coming right up. I'll see you soon."

Jo put down the phone and smiled. She could always count on Kelly for being there for her. She went out on the deck, sorted through her firewood from last year, and found several logs against the house that were not yet wet.

By the time Kelly got there, she had the fire going, warming the house. She opened the door to Kelly, who was soaking wet.

"God, look at you. Come in," Jo said quickly and took the bag from her. "Ever heard of an umbrella?"

"Didn't have enough hands." Kelly laughed and held up the bottle of wine.

Jo met her eyes and smiled. God, she had missed her. Kelly held her gaze and smiled back. Jo finally looked away and went into the kitchen, and Kelly followed.

Jo sat the bag on the counter, took plates down and grabbed a couple of forks, all the while conscious of Kelly watching her. She reached into the cabinet and found two wine glasses, setting them beside the plates. Finally, Jo turned around and faced her.

"The cork screw is in there," she said, pointing to a drawer. She turned back to the plates and began dishing out the rice, chicken and vegetables Kelly had brought.

The cork popped and Kelly reached around her for the glasses, their arms brushing. Jo ignored the thrill that shot through her and put eggrolls on each of their plates before carrying them to the table. Kelly followed with the wine and forks.

"This looks good," Jo said.

Kelly nodded. "Yes."

Jo raised her eyes, one hand resting on the back of the chair. She smiled, then went to Kelly and kissed her quickly on the mouth. "I have missed you," she said softly.

Kelly grinned at her, then sat down, and they ate in silence. After they had cleaned up, they took the bottle of wine and sat by the fire. Jo put on some piano music, turned on a lamp, and sat with Kelly on the sofa.

"If I didn't know better, I'd think you were trying to seduce me," Kelly said.

Jo smiled at her warmly and reached for her hand. "Maybe I am."

Kelly's fingers entwined with hers, and they sat in comfortable silence, listening to the music and watching the fire.

"You must think that I'm terribly difficult," Jo finally said.

Kelly laughed. "Now, why would I think that?"

Jo smiled at her. "Why haven't you been by to see me at school?"

"Honestly?"

"Please."

"I had gotten the feeling that you had only been with me because you needed me, or you needed someone," she said, meeting Jo's eyes. "I didn't think that you were really with me because you wanted me. Just me."

Jo nodded and looked away. Was it true? Had she needed someone? Anyone? No. If that were the case, Deb would have been safer. She didn't have any feelings for Deb.

"So you were waiting for me to call you?" she asked.

"Yes," Kelly admitted. "I felt like I was forcing myself on you."

"No," Jo said. "You just scare me."

"Why do I scare you?" Kelly asked gently.

Jo didn't answer, but she laid her head on Kelly's shoulder. Their fingers still touched, and they were silent.

Finally, Kelly asked, "Are you going to the lake tomorrow?"

"Yes. I need to. I can't keep putting it off."

"Do you want some help?"

Jo nodded.

"We can call Betsy and Janis, too," Kelly suggested.

"Yes, I'm sure they would come."

She didn't want to think about it just now, though. She would call them in the morning.

They sat for awhile longer, watching the fire, then Kelly moved. "I better be going," she said, standing.

Jo wanted her to stay but she knew Kelly wouldn't offer, and Johanna didn't ask. She stood, too.

"Thanks for dinner," she said.

"Anytime." They looked at each other. "Call me in the morning and let me know what time you want to go."

Jo nodded. "Okay."

She walked Kelly to the door, hoping she would take her in her arms and kiss her, but she didn't.

Kelly looked at her for a long moment, her gaze dropping to Jo's lips for only a brief second. "Good night," she said and left.

Jo watched her run to her truck in the rain, then closed the door and leaned against it. After all they had shared, why was it so hard for her? Why couldn't she just go to Kelly and hold her? Why couldn't she just reach up and kiss her? Why couldn't she just ask her to stay? They both wanted it, she knew.

Jo sat on the floor beside the fire and finished her wine. Is this what she wanted? This kind of relationship with Kelly? One where they only stayed together when Jo needed her? What about Kelly's needs? Didn't they matter?

"I'm such a shit," Jo said aloud.

Why Kelly hung around was beyond her. Because she's in love with you, Jo thought, and she closed her eyes to the tears that formed at the idea. Was Kelly driving home now, hurting? Was she wondering why Jo didn't want her?

Later, when Jo crawled into her empty bed, she reached for the phone and called her.

"Kelly?"

"What is it?" she asked.

"I'm sorry."

"Why are you sorry, honey?"

"Because I'm such an ass."

"Don't say that. You just do what you have to do, okay?"

Jo nodded into the phone. "Please don't think that I don't want you. Because I do," she whispered.

"Do you?" Kelly asked.

"Yes."

She could hear Kelly's soft sigh and she smiled.

"I'll see you tomorrow," Kelly said. "Good night."

* * * *

The rain had stopped, but the sky remained cloudy and it was cold out, though not freezing, as had been forecasted. By the time Jo got around to calling Betsy and Janis, it was over forty degrees and the clouds were breaking up, promising sunshine by afternoon.

"Of course we'll help," Betsy agreed. "What time?"

"I'd like to go before lunch," Jo said. "Afterward, we'll go somewhere for an early dinner. My treat."

"Sounds good. Should we meet you there or at your place?"

"Out at the lake, I guess."

Next, she called Kelly. She was waiting.

"Can we take your Explorer? I'd like to bag up his clothes and things and give them to Goodwill."

"Of course. I'll come get you."

Jo waited nervously for her though she didn't know why. Maybe it was because of her admission late last night. Maybe it was just because she was anxious to see her.

Kelly knocked on her door at eleven, wearing faded jeans and a sweatshirt. She looked wonderful.

"Hi," she said, when Jo opened the door.

Jo's eyes looked at her greedily, and she smiled.

"Ready?"

"Let's go."

By eleven-thirty, she was unlocking Harry's door, and it was cold inside. She immediately turned on the heat and went around flipping on lights. Kelly watched her as she walked around, touching the furniture and looking at his things.

"Jo?"

"I'm okay."

And she was. She would give his clothes to Goodwill, where someone less fortunate could use them. What furniture Jo didn't want to keep here, she would offer to the folks at the Senior Center. If they couldn't use it, maybe they'd know someone who could. Unfortunately, there were a lot of Beth's things, as well. Harry had never had the heart to throw them out, and now that was left to Johanna, too.

"Tell me what you want me to do," Kelly said.

"Clothes, I guess."

Jo opened the box of large trash bags she had brought and handed them to Kelly.

"Do you want to look through them first?"

"No. Go ahead," she motioned.

Kelly walked up to her, lifted Jo's face and kissed her lightly on the mouth. Jo smiled, then pushed her into the bedroom.

She was sorting through the books in the living room when Beth and Janis knocked. Jo sent them into the kitchen.

Soon, Harry's and Beth's clothes were piled in the Explorer, and bags of garbage were sitting on the porch. The kitchen was cleaned, the refrigerator nearly empty. They had a box of dry goods Jo was going to give to the local food bank on Monday, and the rest of the cans were left in the pantry.

She gave Harry's few plants to Betsy and Janis. She had enough to worry about with her three.

"You're going to keep the house, then," Betsy said.

"Oh, yes. I couldn't sell it. I've spent too much of my life out here. Besides, I love the lake. I can't imagine not having this to come to anymore."

"You could always live out here during the summer," Janis suggested.

"Yes. I could."

The house was clean, but there was still a lot to sort through. Most of which she would need to do alone.

"I really appreciate your help," she told them.

She and Kelly took the clothes to Goodwill, then drove over to Betsy and Janis's house. They would all ride together to dinner.

"How about seafood?" Jo suggested. "Something different."

"Sure. We could try that new Cajun place on Riverside," Betsy said.

Soon, they were sitting at the Gumbo Pot, sipping cold beer and deciding between shrimp and crawfish for their appetizers.

They had a pleasant dinner. Jo noticed how well Kelly got along with Betsy and Janis, so different from Nancy. Betsy and Nancy had never pretended to like one another, and it had put a strain on their friendship.

After they had dropped Betsy and Janis off, Kelly and Jo rode silently back to Jo's. Kelly pulled in the driveway and left the engine running. Jo looked at her with raised eyebrows. Kelly answered her with the same.

"I wish you'd come in," Jo finally said.

Kelly turned the key, and the truck was silent.

"Actually, I wish you'd stay," Jo admitted.

Kelly reached out and touched her cheek.

"Thank you," she said softly. "I'd love to stay."

Kelly offered to start a fire and Jo went into the kitchen to make them a drink. They sat on the floor by the fire holding hands.

"Today wasn't as hard as I thought it would be."

"No?"

"I'm glad you were there," she said.

Kelly brought her hand up and kissed it softly.

"Do you have plans for Thanksgiving?" Kelly suddenly asked.

"Not really. Susan invited me, but I don't really want to go there."

"Would you like to go to Fredricksburg? Stay in a bed and breakfast?"

Jo looked at her and smiled. "Just us?"

"Just us."

"I think I'd like that."

"I've never been, you know," Kelly admitted.

"To Fredricksburg? Oh, it's a beautiful town. You can do all your Christmas shopping there."

"Shopping?" Kelly grinned. "That's not really what I had in mind," she said, her eyes sparkling with amusement.

"No? And just what did you have in mind?"

"Well, I got a room with a fireplace and a very large bed," she laughed.

Jo smiled at her, set her drink down and went to her. She kissed her full on the mouth, her lips lingering. It had been so long since they had kissed.

"Why don't you show me what you had in mind," she whispered.

Kelly did.

Chapter Twenty-Six

In the weeks before Thanksgiving, Jo had spent a lot of time at Harry's house, throwing away things she didn't want to keep, getting rid of outdated kitchen appliances, and cleaning out cabinets and drawers, which hadn't been done since Beth was alive. She and Kelly had spent a weekend at the lake when it was warm enough for fishing. Jo had gotten her up before dawn and then sped her across the lake to a favorite fishing spot. They caught enough for their dinner, then went back and spent a lazy day on the deck, reading. Kelly's book had been published, and Jo read it in one day, much to Kelly's delight.

"I thought the janitor did it," Jo said.

"The janitor? You were supposed to think the chemistry professor did it. He's the one who knew about the chemicals."

"Janitors have chemicals, too," Jo had insisted. "It was too obvious to be the professor."

"So obvious, it could have been possible."

"I never suspected the wife, of course."

"You weren't supposed to," Kelly preened.

"That's why you're a good writer."

"You think so?"

"Yes, I really do."

They left for Fredricksburg on the Wednesday before Thanksgiving, just after noon, when classes let out. Betsy and Janis had wanted them to spend Thanksgiving at their house, but had conceded that Fredricksburg sounded like fun. Johanna had not told Susan that she and Kelly were going together. She had simply told her that she was going with a friend, that she wanted to get away. Susan had understood.

Now, as they sped through the Hill Country, Jo laid her hand on Kelly's thigh and smiled. They had had a good two weeks. Kelly had stayed with her a couple of nights each week, but only when Jo asked. When they made love, it was as intense as ever, but they didn't speak. Kelly didn't have to. Jo could see it all in her eyes.

"I'm glad we're going," Jo said.

"Me, too. It'll be good to get away."

"Yes."

"What did you usually do on Thanksgiving?" Kelly asked.

"Harry cooked enough to feed a family of ten," she said and laughed. "Last year, Betsy and Janis joined us, too."

"We could have stayed with them, then come up here on Friday," Kelly reminded her.

"No. I'd rather be here with you." And it was true.

When they drove into Fredricksburg, the streets were crowded with tourists.

"I thought this was a small town," Kelly complained.

Jo laughed. "It is. It swells during the holidays. Look at all the arts and crafts shops we can explore."

"Can't wait," Kelly said with a grimace.

They checked into their room, which overlooked Main Street, now crowded with cars and people. They looked at the king-sized bed and smiled at each other. Firewood was ready in the fireplace and there was a neat stack just outside their door.

They unpacked their things, then went outside to join the others, walking the streets already decorated for Christmas. They strolled close together, their shoulders brushing, eyes meeting often. Jo wished they could walk holding hands, as others did around them. Their steps were lazy, and Jo was content just window shopping, but occasionally she would drag Kelly into a shop when something caught her eye. Hours later, when they found a small tavern, Jo's side of the booth was crowded with packages. They drank large frosty mugs of draft beer while they waited for their chicken-fried steaks. Jo was aware that they could barely keep their eyes off one another.

“You made quite a haul,” Kelly teased.

“Okay, I confess. I love to shop.”

“Oh? So the allure this weekend was shopping?”

Jo met her eyes. “Actually, the allure was you.” Then she grinned. “Shopping was just a bonus.”

Afterward, they walked back to their room, silently. The streets were less crowded, and they paused several times to admire the Christmas lights.

“Looks like a postcard,” Kelly observed.

"Yes. All we need is snow."

By the time they reached their room, the night air had cooled.

"You can shower first," Kelly offered. "I'll start a fire."

Later, they turned the lights out and sat by the fire on the floor. Kelly leaned back against the sofa and drew Jo to her. They kissed softly, quietly, and drew back. Their eyes met in the glow of the fire and they smiled.

"Having fun?" Kelly asked.

"Yes. This was a wonderful idea."

Kelly nodded. "And I get you to myself for three whole days."

Jo laughed. "I knew that was your intention all along. I just knew you didn't really want to go shopping."

Kelly cupped Jo's face in her hands. "I really want to make love to you," she whispered.

Jo met her lips urgently. Kelly set their wine aside and pulled Jo to her feet. She slowly pulled Jo's shirt over her head and touched her breasts. Jo stood there, eyes closed, heart pounding.

In the quiet glow of the fire, they kissed and caressed their clothes away. Kelly's kiss was like the sweet taste of winter wine, and Jo drank her fill, exploring Kelly's mouth with her own.

But Kelly's hands grew impatient. She knelt on the rug, tugging Jo down with her. On their knees, they embraced, urgent hands touching, arousing.

Jo lay back, her arms reaching for Kelly, pulling her weight on top of her, and Jo opened her legs, letting Kelly settle between them.

"I love being with you, Jo," Kelly whispered into her mouth.

Kelly supported herself with her arms, pressing her hips into Jo, straining to touch her, wetness against wetness.

Jo circled Kelly's hips with her legs, opening wider, wanting to draw Kelly inside her. She heard Kelly's subtle change in breathing, gasps coming through her parted lips as their hips rolled together, again and again.

"Yes," Jo breathed. "Come for me."

Her hips rose up, meeting each of Kelly's thrusts, now harder. She felt Kelly tremble in her arms, and she watched Kelly's face contort and strain as each breath tore from her. The muscles in Kelly's arms stood out with each roll of her hips, and Jo again rose up to meet her.

"Come on," Jo whispered.

Kelly's hips now writhed against Jo, faster and faster, until at last Kelly groaned deep in her throat, one last thrust, then another, finally collapsing on top Jo.

Their bodies damp with perspiration, they lay together in the glow of the fire, and Jo soothed Kelly's back with gentle hands.

"Okay?"

"Mmm."

Kelly rolled off her, resting on her side as her leg still pinned Jo to the rug. Her mouth went to Jo's breast as her hand slipped between Jo's thighs.

"Oh, you're so wet," she murmured.

Kelly cradled Jo's head on her arm, her lips moving back to Jo's mouth. Her thigh nudged Jo's legs farther apart. Her tongue was hot inside Jo's mouth, and Kelly's fingers moved through Jo's wetness, slipping inside her, letting Jo set the rhythm as her hips rose and fell, pulsing against Kelly's fingers.

"Yes," Jo breathed. "Harder."

Kelly moved over her, her fingers diving deep inside Jo, thrusting into her wetness. Then she moved down, her mouth joining her fingers, sucking Jo hotly into her mouth as her fingers delved deeper still.

"Kelly!" Jo cried, and her hands in Kelly's hair forced her mouth down hard. She cried Kelly's name again and again as her orgasm ripped through her, and she screamed with pleasure.

"Dear God," she gasped. "Come here."

She pulled Kelly on top of her and held her. She was trembling but she couldn't help it. Each time, she felt like she would explode from the feelings surging through her.

They lay quietly until Jo's breathing finally slowed. She brushed Kelly's hair softly, again and again, her eyes closed.

"Okay, honey?" Kelly finally asked, and Jo smiled at her endearment.

"Very much okay."

They rolled over, and this time, Jo pinned Kelly with her leg. She kissed Kelly's cheek lightly and smiled. It was very much okay, indeed.

"My turn," she sighed into Kelly's ear as her tongue slipped inside. She was always filled with such a need to please Kelly, and Jo let her body slide over her. Lovemaking had never been this way before. It had always seemed hurried and rushed. With Kelly, it was anything but that. Jo took her time as her lips touched Kelly's face, her eyes, her nose before finding her waiting lips. Their kiss was hot and wet, and their tongues danced together.

Jo pressed her thigh hard between Kelly's legs, feeling Kelly's wetness and rubbing against it. Kelly's legs opened wider, and she arched into Jo's leg, her hips rising and falling in rhythm. Jo's mouth found Kelly's breast, the nipple hard and swollen, and she took first one, then the other into her mouth. Kelly held her tight, her hands pressing Jo closer. Jo's mouth opened, and her tongue teased the taut peak before sucking the nipple into her mouth again, and Kelly moaned with pleasure, her hands on Jo's face.

Jo's hand moved down Kelly's body, and she quickly slid her fingers deep inside her.

"Oh, God, yes," Kelly breathed, and her hips pushed up hard, shoving Jo deeper inside. Jo moved quickly in and out, plunging her fingers deep into Kelly's wetness and Kelly stilled, already near orgasm.

But Jo wasn't nearly through and she quickly pulled away and again pressed her thigh between Kelly's legs, her mouth still at her breast.

"Jo, please," Kelly begged her.

"I want to taste you."

Jo moved down slowly, her mouth open as she pushed Kelly's legs apart. Kelly was so wet, and Jo's tongue moved into her, over her, and her lips took Kelly into her mouth. Jo's arms wrapped under Kelly's legs, holding her tightly as her tongue stroked Kelly to orgasm. Kelly cried out loudly, and Jo pressed her face down into her, her cheeks wet with her.

Kelly's legs fell limply to the rug. She reached for Jo and slowly pulled her up. "I love you," she whispered.

Jo lay still, her heart hammering in her chest at Kelly's words. She had known it, of course. She just didn't want to hear it. As the light of the fire danced over them, Jo shook her head slowly and squeezed her eyes shut.

"Jo, I can't keep pretending that I don't," she insisted.

"I'm not sure I want you to love me."

"But I do. I'm very much in love with you. It's never been like this with anyone before," she whispered.

She held Jo tightly to her.

"Please don't say that."

"It's true, honey."

"Kelly, I can't let myself love you," she said. "Everyone I've ever loved is gone. Everyone who's ever loved me is gone."

"I'm not going anywhere," Kelly promised and brushed at the tears that escaped Jo's eyes.

Jo said nothing. What could she say? She desired Kelly, yes. She enjoyed being with her. She admitted that she needed her, but love? No, she couldn't let herself love Kelly. She wouldn't.

"Should we stop seeing each other?" Kelly asked.

"No. I don't want that," Jo said quickly.

"Maybe this is too much, too soon. Maybe we need to spend more time alone or with other people," Kelly said quietly.

"God," Jo whispered. "I don't want that. I'm sorry. I know I'm being difficult, Kelly. I want to be with you."

"Deb has shown an interest in you. Maybe you need to pursue that," Kelly continued.

"And Lucy has shown an interest in you."

"Honey, I don't want Lucy."

"Then why are you doing this?"

"I think you need to ask yourself why you're with me. Is this all you want? A physical relationship with no strings attached?"

"I don't know what I want," Jo admitted.

Kelly let out a weary sigh. "Then I certainly don't know either."

Chapter Twenty-Seven

They got home before noon on Sunday. It had been a busy weekend. Thursday, they had joined other tourists at a local beer joint to watch football games and then went to the nicest restaurant they could find for turkey dinner. Friday and Saturday, Jo dragged Kelly with her through the shops and completed her Christmas shopping. They finished early enough Saturday to take a quick trip to Enchanted Rock, where they hiked the giant granite mound and crawled through the caves at the top. Kelly had been there camping the summer before, but Jo had not been there since her high school days.

Home, Kelly helped Jo unload her things and put all her packages on the sofa.

"Did you buy me anything?" Kelly asked.

"Now, you're not supposed to ask that. Besides, when would I have had a chance? You were with me the whole time."

"Yeah, well, I bought you something," Kelly teased.

"You did? What?"

"It's a present. You'll have to wait," she said with a grin.

Jo looked at her for a moment, then went into her arms. "Thank you for taking me. I had a wonderful time."

Kelly kissed her gently on the forehead. "I enjoyed our time together."

"I'm sorry about. . . ."

"Don't. We agreed not to talk about it. So let's not," Kelly said. "I'll see you tomorrow at school."

Jo watched her go and stood staring at the road a long time after her truck had disappeared. They had agreed not to talk about it, but it was there between them. Their lovemaking had become more guarded. The love Jo had seen in Kelly's eyes was hidden now. Is this how Jo wanted it? Just a physical relationship? That's all it had become the last few days. There were no touches, other than in bed. During the days, they had been merely friends, no intimate looks passed between them.

Kelly had suggested they spend some time apart, and judging by the way she had left today, that's what was going to happen. Jo felt miserable. Her heart ached, and she didn't know why.

There were only three more weeks of classes, the last four days of that being finals. It had been a long semester, and Jo would be thankful when it finally ended.

She was behind in all of her classes, and she stayed at the college most evenings until seven. It was to catch up and get her finals organized, at least that's what she told herself, but she knew it was to keep her mind off Kelly. She had barely seen her all week. Kelly complained of being busy, too, and Jo believed her. What else could she do?

On Thursday, Jo called her in her office.

"Do you want to have dinner?"

There was a long pause. "I can't," Kelly said.

"Why not?" Jo asked.

"I've already got plans this evening."

"Oh. I see."

"How about Saturday?" Kelly asked. "Maybe we could get Betsy and Janis to join us."

Jo wondered if she already had plans for Friday night, too, but she didn't ask. "Okay. I'll call them."

"Let me know," Kelly said and hung up.

Jo replaced the receiver slowly and stared at the phone for a moment. This was what she wanted, she stubbornly told herself.

She spent a lonely Friday night by the fire, a bottle of wine beside her. It was nearly empty, and the book she had started lay opened to the first chapter. She stared into the fire, wondering what Kelly was doing and with whom. It was the "with whom" that bothered her. Lucy? Perhaps. Or maybe someone from San Antonio. Jo leaned her head back, and jealousy consumed her. The thought of Kelly being with someone else was like a knife ripping through her heart, shredding what was left of it.

She finished the wine, knowing she would have a terrible headache in the morning and not caring in the least. Betsy and Janis had agreed to dinner, and Jo had tried calling Kelly but she wasn't home. She didn't leave a message.

Jo slept until nine on Saturday morning, and as she stood, her head reminded her she had consumed an entire bottle of wine by herself. She sat at the table, drinking coffee and watching the birds at her feeder, which was full for once.

She stared at the phone, wishing it would ring, but it remained silent. Finally, she called Kelly and got her answering machine again.

"It's Jo. Betsy and Janis said dinner would be fine. If you still want to, that is," she added. "I guess about seven."

She hung up and went back to her coffee, a lonely day looming ahead of her.

Kelly called at four.

"Seven?" she asked.

"Yes."

"Okay, that's fine," Kelly agreed.

"Do you want to come here first?" Jo asked.

"No. I better just meet you there. I've got some things to do this afternoon."

Jo bit her lip and nodded. "Okay," she said and hung up.

"God, I hate this," Jo said out loud.

She went to their house about six. She couldn't stand being alone a second longer. They were surprised to see her.

"Jo, come in," Betsy said.

"I know I'm early," she admitted.

"Where's Kelly?"

"She's meeting us here."

"What's wrong?" Betsy asked immediately.

"Why do you think something's wrong?"

Betsy raised her eyebrows. "Because I know you, that's why." She led her into the living room. "Let's talk."

"You're not even dressed yet."

"I've showered. Janis is getting ready," Betsy said. "Now, what's wrong?"

"I don't know."

"You don't know?"

"Well, I know what's wrong, I just don't know why," Jo complained.

"Fredricksburg went okay?"

"Yes and no," she said.

Betsy just looked at her, waiting for her to continue.

"We had a good time, I guess." Jo looked away. "Oh, Betsy, I just don't know. I like being with her, but she wants more. I told her I couldn't. That I wanted things to stay the way they were."

"Which is what? Strictly physical? Sexual?"

Jo nodded.

"And?"

"And she said that maybe we needed to stop spending so much time together. Maybe we needed to see other people since I wasn't ready for anything more with her."

Betsy didn't say anything.

"I've barely seen her this week. I asked her to dinner Thursday and she had plans and I guess last night, too. She didn't even want to come to my house tonight. She said she would meet me here," she finished in a rush.

"And this isn't what you want?"

"I don't know what the hell I want," Jo said.

"I think you do, but you just won't admit it," Betsy said quietly.

"No." Jo shook her head.

"You obviously enjoy your time with her," Betsy said with a slight smile.

Jo blushed. "Yes. The sex is beyond compare. But I don't want more."

"You don't want her, but you don't want anyone else to, either?"

"Betsy, she told me she loved me," Jo whispered.

"And you freaked?"

Jo nodded.

"Honey, I wish I could tell you what to do. I know you feel something for her."

"I like her a lot, yes. But I don't love her. I don't want to love her," Jo insisted.

"Maybe you forgot to tell your heart that," Betsy said quietly.

"No," Jo said stubbornly. "We enjoy each other, yes. But I'm not in love with her."

"Okay, if you say so. You should know." Betsy looked at her for a long moment. "Then what's wrong? It shouldn't bother you if she goes out with someone else."

"It shouldn't, should it?"

"No."

Jo nodded.

"Get yourself a beer. I've got to get dressed."

Kelly didn't get there until five minutes before seven, and they were waiting for her. Jo searched her eyes but Kelly's rested on hers for only a brief second.

"Hi everyone," she said. "Sorry I'm late."

"We're just having a beer. Want one?" Janis asked.

"Yes, please."

She avoided the sofa where Jo was and sat in the armchair across from her. "How did your week go?' she asked.

"Busy," Jo said.

"Mine, too. It just flew by."

Jo wished she could say the same. Kelly was wearing slacks and a sweater, and Jo found herself staring at her full breasts where the sweater hugged them. She had to tear her eyes away.

"Do you two have plans for Christmas?" Janis asked.

"I'll be going to California," Kelly said, and Jo felt her heart sink. Would Kelly be gone the entire time?

"Oh, that's right. Your family is out there."

"Yeah. What will you do?" she asked.

"Oh, we only have a few days off. Betsy's mother always comes and stays, though."

"We bought your book, by the way," Betsy said. "I loved it. Janis just started it."

"And don't tell me a thing. I think the janitor did it," Janis said.

Jo and Kelly glanced at each other and smiled.

They went for Mexican food, and Jo had two margaritas. She ordered the second after Kelly mentioned that she had been at the bar the night before.

"Deb was there," she told Jo. "She said to tell you hello if I saw you."

"How nice," Jo said and forced a smile. That meant Lucy was there, as well. Had she danced with her? Of course. Had she taken her home? Jo refused to think about that.

"We could go out tonight, if you want," Janis offered.

"No. I'm really tired. You all go if you want, though. Don't mind me," Kelly said.

Why was she tired? Had she made love long into the night and early morning? Jo felt her heart tighten, and she bit her bottom lip hard.

Once back at their house, Kelly came in for only a minute. "I've got to get going. I've got some work to do in the morning. Thanks for dinner. I enjoyed it."

She turned to Jo. "I guess I'll see you at school."

"I guess," Jo said and shrugged.

Kelly met her eyes and started to say something else, then looked away and was gone.

"Jesus, what's with you two?" Janis asked.

"I haven't had a chance to tell her," Betsy said to Jo.

"Tell me what?"

"I'll leave you two to discuss my personal life in private," Jo said and stood up.

"Are you okay?" Betsy asked.

"No. I don't guess that I am."

She cried on the way home. It was the margaritas, she supposed. Tequila always depressed her.

"Who are you kidding?" she demanded aloud as she wiped her cheeks. God, she missed Kelly.

Her answering machine was blinking when she got home, and she pushed the button as she walked past.

"Jo, please call me when you get in."

Jo stared at the machine, wondering what Kelly wanted. She thought briefly that she wouldn't call her, but she knew she would.

She got ready for bed, and as she lay there in the dark, she reached for the phone. Kelly answered right away.

"It's me," Jo said.

"Hi."

"What is it?" she asked.

Kelly was silent for a moment. "I wanted to tell you that I missed you," she said quietly.

"Do you?" Jo asked coldly.

"Yes."

"Is that why you went out last night?"

"Yes, it is," Kelly said.

Jo closed her eyes and she felt tears well there. "Was Lucy there?"

"Yes, she was," Kelly admitted.

"Did you dance with her?"

"Yes."

"Slow songs?" she whispered.

"Yes."

Jo felt a tear escape. "Did you kiss her?"

Kelly paused for only a moment. "She kissed me, yes."

Jo bit her lip as tears fell from her eyes. Her heart lodged in her throat, and she swallowed hard.

"Jo?"

"Why?" Jo asked with a sob. "Why are you doing this?"

"You don't want me."

"I want you," Jo insisted.

"You don't want me the way I need you to want me."

"And Lucy does?"

Kelly didn't answer.

"Please tell me you didn't spend the night with her. I couldn't stand it if you did," she said softly and let her tears fall.

"No, I didn't spend the night with her."

"Did you spend part of the night with her?"

"Jo, don't do this," she warned.

"Oh, God. You slept with her, didn't you?" Jo closed her eyes and pictured them together, and she thought she was going to be sick.

"I was drunk enough to, I guess, but no, I didn't sleep with her. I left alone."

"You hurt me," Jo whispered.

"I don't mean to," Kelly whispered back.

"Why won't you talk to me anymore?"

"You don't think it hurts me to be with you? To feel the way I do about you and know that nothing can come of it?"

"I'm so sorry," Jo cried. "I miss you."

"Jo, what do you want from me?" Kelly asked. "You don't want my love. Do you just want sex?"

"Please, don't."

"Goddamn it, Jo." She hung up.

Jo replaced the phone gently, rolled over and cried.

Jo didn't leave the house on Sunday, and she didn't answer the phone. The weather matched her mood, cold and rainy all day long. She forced herself to read, and she forced herself to cook dinner, although she ended up throwing most of it away.

Betsy and Janis called and invited her to a movie, but she didn't return their call. Kelly called, too. Twice. But Jo didn't return her calls, either.

Monday morning, Kelly was waiting beside her office door. Jo wouldn't meet her eyes and Kelly followed her inside and closed the door behind her.

"You didn't return my calls," she accused.

"You hung up on me," Jo shot back.

"I'm in love with you," Kelly said.

Jo closed her eyes and turned away. She didn't need this so early in the morning.

"But I think I can get past that," Kelly said.

Jo turned back to her. "What?"

"I also need you. And I think you need me," she continued. "I know you don't love me. You may never love me."

Jo saw the hurt in her eyes.

"But that's okay. I did a lot of thinking yesterday. I'd rather be with you the way things were then to not be with you at all."

"Kelly," Jo whispered. She felt tears sting her eyes again, and she moved to turn away. Kelly grabbed her arm and turned her around.

"Don't you even want that anymore?" Kelly demanded.

"Yes, I want that. You're right. I do need you," she whispered. "It's just that I'm so mixed up, and I've been so goddamned miserable."

Kelly took her in her arms, and Jo held on tightly. Yes, she needed Kelly. She had been so afraid she would never know her arms again. She closed her eyes, laid her head on Kelly's shoulder and cried.

"Shhh. I'm sorry," Kelly whispered. "I won't say it again, I promise. Who knows, maybe it will go away."

Jo nodded and held her and wished she had called her back yesterday.

"Can I come over tonight?" Kelly asked.

Jo nodded and pulled out of her arms.

"I'll bring a pizza."

Chapter Twenty-Eight

They made love that night with as much intensity as they ever had. Jo cried afterward and Kelly held her, wiping her tears as they fell.

"What is it?" Kelly asked.

"I've missed you so much," Jo said. "I just couldn't bear to think that you were making love to Lucy."

"Lucy?"

"Thursday night. Friday night. I was so alone Friday night. I just knew that you were with her. And you were."

"I wasn't with her, Jo. She and Deb were at the bar. I danced with her. I danced with Deb, too."

"Did Deb kiss you, too?" Jo asked, and she smiled.

"No."

"Did you dance with Lucy like you dance with me?" she asked seriously.

Kelly pushed her down and pinned Jo with her leg. "And just how do I dance with you?"

"Like you can't wait to take me home and make love to me."

"Oh." Kelly kissed her gently. "Then, no, I didn't dance with Lucy like that." She smiled against Jo's lips. "In fact, there was at least two feet between us at all times."

"I just bet. How did she get close enough to kiss you then?"

"Well, she held me against that back wall. It's very dark back there and before I knew what was happening. . . ."

"Don't," Jo said and covered Kelly's mouth with her own. "I don't want to hear it."

"Then why did you ask?"

"You kissed her back, didn't you?"

"What if I told you I was pretending it was you?"

"Were you?"

"Yes. Only she doesn't kiss nearly as well as you do."

"I don't like to think of you kissing her," Jo said.

"Then don't. I didn't really kiss her, you know. We were dancing. A little closer than the two feet that I mentioned," she admitted, laying her head on Jo's shoulder. "She ambushed me, really. I was drinking too much and my mind was wandering. I was thinking about you and how I should be with you."

"Were you really?"

"Really. Anyway, before I knew it, she was trying to shove her tongue down my throat."

"Oh, Kelly," Jo groaned.

Kelly laughed. "I shouldn't have even been there. I don't even know why I went out."

"Why did you?" Jo asked.

Kelly stared into her eyes. "I was trying to get you out of my mind. The bar seemed like a good place to start."

Jo touched Kelly's face lightly. "And Lucy was there."

"I shouldn't have danced with her. It's unfair to her, you know. I don't like to think that I was leading her on."

"Were you?"

"No. I wasn't. You're the only one I want to be with, Jo."

Jo kissed her full on the mouth. "I want to be with you, too." Jo pulled Kelly on top of her. "Make love to me again," she whispered.

Kelly spent nearly every night with Jo from then on. Sometimes, she would bring clothes for the next day, and sometimes she would leave early and go to her apartment to shower and change. She never again told Jo that she loved her, and her eyes never told Jo either. When they made love, Jo had to initiate it. Even then, Kelly felt distant from her, her mind elsewhere. They never spoke of the pleasure that they gave each other and Jo was very conscious that things had changed between them. Many nights, Kelly fell asleep almost instantly, barely kissing Jo good night. Jo would wake in her arms, though, having moved to her in the darkness.

During the day, they were just friends. They had lunch together often, sometimes out, or sometimes Kelly would pick up sandwiches to eat in Jo's office. They both worked late most nights. Papers needed grading and finals needed to be written.

And this was the way Jo wanted it, she told herself. No words of love were spoken between them, and they had no commitment. Just a physical relationship, just like Jo had requested. It was all she needed, she insisted.

But was it really?

One night, in the middle of December, they sat on the floor beside the fire and held hands, their dinner plates pushed aside. Jo caressed Kelly's palm with her thumb, moving it slowly, gently against her. Kelly made no move to touch her, instead, her hand remained still, her fingers limp.

Jo stopped and looked at her. Kelly was staring into the fire, her thoughts far away.

"What's wrong?" Jo finally asked.

Kelly turned to her, her eyes veiled. "Nothing."

"You haven't wanted me for awhile now," Jo said. "Why?"

"Is that what you think?"

Jo nodded and looked away. "It's my fault, I know."

"Please don't think that. I want you more than I ever have," Kelly insisted.

"It hasn't been the same."

"The same as when?"

"Before," Jo said simply.

"I made you a promise," Kelly said quietly. "When I'm with you like that, I have a hard time keeping that promise."

Jo went to her and kissed her on the mouth. "You've been so far away from me."

"I've been right here," Kelly said and touched Jo's breast, over her heart.

"Make love to me like before," Jo pleaded, her eyes looking into Kelly's, searching for the love that had once been there.

"You said that you. . . ."

"Shhh," Jo whispered, her fingers covering Kelly's mouth. "Just make love to me."

Kelly kissed her gently, her lips soft and slow. She raised her eyes and Jo melted under their power. They hid nothing.

Kelly pulled her to her feet and led her into the bedroom. She undressed Jo slowly, her hands warm where they touched. She bent her head and touched her lips to Jo's breast, then found her mouth waiting. Jo urgently pulled at

Kelly's clothes and soon they were naked, their eyes traveling over each other.

Kelly moved to turn the light out, but Jo stopped her.

"No, leave it on. I want to see you."

Kelly laid down and pulled Jo after her, and their mouths met, not gently, but with a hunger that had been missing for so long. Jo thrilled to the touch of Kelly's hands again as they held her possessively. Jo's tongue pushed into Kelly's mouth, and she tasted every part of her, pulling out slowly, only to go back for more.

Kelly's hands moved over Jo, pulling her snugly against her, her legs opening as Jo's hips pushed against her. They lay together, their breasts touching, and Jo rubbed against her.

"I want you so much," Jo breathed into her mouth, her voice husky with desire.

"I'm all yours," Kelly whispered.

Jo captured Kelly's hands and moved them above her head, holding them there on the pillow. Her tongue snaked into Kelly's ear, wetting it, then moved over her neck, kissing her throat where the pulse beat rapidly. Jo paused for a moment and looked at Kelly, so desirable, her eyes shut, her lips slightly parted as her breath came quickly.

Jo lay on her side, one leg pressed hard between Kelly's thighs, her mouth settled over one of Kelly's breasts, her tongue touching the nipple, feeling it swell against her lips. Kelly moaned softly and tried to free her hands, but Jo held them tight, her mouth hungrily sucking at Kelly's breast.

"I want to touch you," Kelly pleaded.

"No," Jo murmured. "Let me have my way with you."

Kelly groaned as Jo moved to her other breast, then back to her lips. Jo know she would never tire of making love to this woman who was so responsive to her touch. She drew back and their eyes met. Kelly closed hers slowly as Jo reached up and caressed her face, thumbs gently touching Kelly's lips.

"It's never been like this before. No one's ever made me feel the way you do," Kelly whispered and opened her eyes, and Jo acknowledged the love that she saw there.

"For me either," Jo admitted, and she kissed Kelly's mouth again.

Then she straddled Kelly, letting Kelly feel her wetness as she kept Kelly's arms pinned above her head. She dipped her head, teasing Kelly's nipples with her tongue, causing Kelly to squirm under her. She moved down Kelly's body. She could wait no longer.

Jo pushed Kelly's legs apart gently with her hands, and she could see how ready Kelly was for her. She wanted her mouth there. Her tongue reached out and touched Kelly, sliding through her wetness, tasting her, and Kelly let her breath out, a low moan escaping her.

"Oh, Jo," she breathed, and Jo saw her hands reach for the headboard.

Jo's breath came fast, and she pushed Kelly's thighs up with her shoulders, and her mouth covered her, her tongue sliding into her, warm and soft and wet. She could love her this way all night, she thought, and her eyes closed as she moved over her, into her, her tongue moving fast against her. Much too soon, Kelly's hips rose, and Jo moved even faster until Kelly cried out, her legs trembling with orgasm.

Kelly's legs fell limp to the bed, and Jo kissed her thighs gently, then kissed her soft mound of hair again and crawled up beside her. She gathered Kelly in her arms and held her, her own eyes closed as her heart slowed.

"Jo, I love you so much," Kelly whispered. "I ache from it."

"I don't want to hurt you," Jo said. She opened her eyes and watched Kelly, her eyes still shut.

"I wish you could trust me."

Jo felt her own heart ache. Kelly's brow was drawn, and Jo saw her squeeze her eyes tighter, saw the tears that escaped anyway. Tears she had caused. She reached up and kissed them away, her tongue drying them as they fell.

"Please don't cry," Jo whispered.

"I love you."

"I know you do," she said gently.

Jo wanted to say the words back to her, though she dared not. She surely felt like her own heart would burst if she didn't, for she knew she was in love with Kelly. She had been for a very long time, she admitted now. But saying the words out loud was more than she could allow. Admitting them to herself was scary enough. Saying them to Kelly would change everything. It would make their relationship real. It would mean commitment.

Kelly opened her eyes and stared into Jo's for a very long time. Jo didn't look away. Kelly finally drew her down to kiss her.

"I'm sorry."

"Please don't say you're sorry," Jo whispered. "I..."

She stopped before the words rushed out and she closed her eyes, so afraid Kelly would see the love there.

"Let me make love to you," Kelly said as she rolled over, pinning Jo beneath her.

Jo smiled and guided Kelly's mouth to hers. Yes, she could show her love that way. She could tell Kelly she loved her by her actions, if not by her words.

Kelly's mouth slowly assaulted her, and Jo lay back, her eyes closed to the light as the feel of Kelly's tongue and mouth dissolved her. Her own tongue drew Kelly's into her mouth, and she held her near, her hands on her face holding her close. She had never wanted another person as much as she wanted Kelly. She was consumed with desire for her. Wrapping her arms around her, she held her tightly.

Kelly pulled away and watched her. Jo closed her eyes again, afraid of what they might reveal. Her hands slowly moved over Kelly's back and she pulled Kelly to her breast.

Kelly's mouth found her, sucking her nipple, causing Jo to rise up to meet her mouth. Kelly's mouth opened, and her hand squeezed Jo's breast, and Jo let her breath out slowly as Kelly's tongue licked at her nipple.

"Oh, yes," she breathed and held Kelly there for a long time.

Kelly moved her hand down between them, her fingers searching for Jo's wetness, and she glided into her, her fingers moving over her.

"Tell me what you want," Kelly whispered.

"I want to feel your mouth on me," Jo sighed.

Kelly covered Jo's mouth with her own and slowly slipped her tongue inside. "Like this?" she asked.

"Yes, just like that."

Kelly pushed Jo's legs apart with her thighs and pressed her hips into her, and Jo rose to meet her, wanting to touch her. Kelly slowly slid down her body, her tongue stroking as she went, wetting her. Jo waited patiently, her breast heaving with each breath she took as Kelly's mouth went lower.

"Please," she begged, when Kelly paused to kiss her hips.

Jo opened her legs, longing for Kelly to settle between them, and her hands pushed Kelly's shoulders, urging her to hurry. She couldn't stand another moment of this sweet torment.

Kelly continued to make her wait though, her lips moving over Jo's thighs and down her legs.

"Kelly, I'm dying," she moaned.

"We can't have that." Kelly spread Jo's legs even farther apart.

Jo's eyes squeezed shut when finally, finally, she felt Kelly touch her with her tongue, lightly, teasing.

"God, you're driving me insane," Jo breathed.

Kelly's hands circled Jo's thighs, and Jo held her breath as Kelly finally took her. Kelly's mouth opened over her, and her tongue moved inside of her, and Jo pressed back into the bed, then rose up to meet her, feeling Kelly's tongue move in and out. God, yes, this was what she wanted. This was what she needed.

Kelly's lips moved over her, her mouth and tongue stroking her as Jo writhed beneath her, her hips moving frantically as her orgasm threatened, but it was too soon. She wasn't nearly ready for this to end, and she held her breath, wanting it to last for hours, but she felt the first wave of orgasm swallow her, and her hips stilled, her feet pushed hard into the bed as she cried out, her hands clutching Kelly's shoulders, pressing her hard against her.

Oh, I do love you, she thought. She laid back, spent, and her arms dropped to her sides. She felt Kelly move beside her, and she turned her head and looked into her eyes.

"Oh, honey, that was wonderful," Jo whispered.

Kelly's eyes darkened at the endearment, and Jo closed her own and smiled.

Their lovemaking was like before. Long into the early morning hours, they touched. Sleep claimed them briefly, but they woke and made love again and again, until the sun rose, casting shadows around them as they held each other.

Chapter Twenty-Nine

Kelly left for San Francisco on the twenty-second. Jo cried when she dropped her off at the airport, as much for her being gone as for the words she said. And those that Jo did not say.

"I wish we could be together," Kelly said, as they sat quietly in Jo's car.

"I'll miss you."

Kelly cupped Jo's face and rubbed her lips gently with her thumb and smiled so sweetly that Jo was certain she would burst into tears right there.

"I really love you, Jo."

"I know," Jo acknowledged.

Kelly simply nodded and was gone, and Jo was left staring after her, wishing she had told her, but still so afraid. Afraid of what? It wasn't like it wasn't true. It wasn't like it would hurt any less if they ended their relationship, just because she had not said the words. What she had felt for Nancy couldn't even compare with what she felt for Kelly. After all these years, she finally knew what Harry and Beth had had together. A love so powerful that it consumed you, brought you to your knees with its strength, scared you.

She drove back to her empty house, wiping the occasional tear from her cheek. Kelly had asked Jo to go to California with her, but she wasn't ready to meet her family, so she had accepted Betsy's invitation to spend Christmas with them. Now, she wished she had been stronger, wished she had agreed to go with Kelly.

When she returned home, she found a small, wrapped gift sitting on top of her table. She had not seen Kelly put it there. She had assumed they would exchange gifts when she returned. She went to it now and smiled at Kelly's scribbled note.

Don't open until Christmas!

Jo held it to her breast with her eyes shut, feeling a swell of love surge through her.

"You're such a fool," she scolded herself. "Such a fool."

She took the gift and put it under her tree beside the ones she had gotten for Betsy and Janis. She would wait, like Kelly had requested, but she couldn't resist a quick shake of the box. The movement inside gave her no clue as to its contents, and she felt like a child sneaking into the presents a week before Christmas.

On Christmas Eve, she went to Betsy and Janis's early. Betsy was out shopping with her mother, so she had offered to help Janis cook their traditional Christmas meal of turkey with all the fixings. Actually, Jo was looking forward to it.

What they had eaten in Fredricksburg could hardly be called "traditional," and it always tasted so much better when you spent the better part of the day cooking it.

"How're you holding up?" Janis asked.

"I'm fine," Jo said, and she was. Being without Harry was much easier when she had such good friends.

"Have you talked to Kelly?" Janis asked a short time later.

"No, she hasn't called."

She had tried to put it from her mind, the fact that Kelly had not called her. She was sure she was busy with her family and friends back home and had little time to dwell on her. Kelly had left her parents' number with Jo, but Jo had refused to call, as much as she wanted to.

"How are things with you?"

"Okay."

Jo stopped peeling the potato in her hand and turned to Janis. "I guess. I'm very difficult. Kelly must have the patience of a saint."

"Love can give you patience, if nothing else," Janis said with a laugh. "Look how long I've endured Betsy's mother for Christmas. Every year, there's always something wrong. The turkey's too dry, the dressing is too moist, the pies are overdone, the tree's too big, too small. I could go on and on." She sighed.

Jo smiled, knowing very well how difficult Betsy's mother could be. Maybe that was why Betsy only saw her once a year. Betsy's mother had not quite accepted Janis into the family, even after all these years.

"You are staying the night, aren't you?" Janis asked.

"I think I will, if the invitation is still open."

"Of course. We'd love for you to. Besides, you give me a buffer against Madge."

That night, long after the dinner dishes were put up and the others were asleep, Jo let her thoughts drift to Kelly. She had kept them at bay throughout the evening, but now she closed her eyes, snuggled under the covers, and let images of Kelly wash over her. Oh, she missed her terribly. Not just at night, either. She missed talking to her, she missed looking at her. She missed her smile, her voice, her smell. She missed all of her, and when she got back, Jo vowed to tell her just how much she missed her.

She heard the coffee pot click on at six, but the others were not yet stirring. She tossed the covers off and hurried to the bathroom she shared with Madge to take a quick shower. She was just pouring her first cup of coffee when Betsy walked in.

"You're up early," she said.

"Wanted to beat the rush."

"Have you opened it yet?" Betsy asked with a smile.

Jo grinned. "No. I didn't sneak a peak during the night, if that's what you mean."

After everyone had filled their coffee cups, they settled around the tree, and Janis passed out the few gifts that were there. Jo saved Kelly's for last, although she was dying to open it first.

Madge got her a sweater, and Jo thanked her, then laughed when Madge opened up a similar sweater from Jo. Betsy and Janis had gotten her a couple of CDs and a gift certificate from her favorite clothing store. She got them a painting from a local artist and a ceramic doll for Janis's collection. They particularly enjoyed the painting of Lake Travis and were already deciding where to hang it. While they were opening the rest of their gifts from Madge, Jo reached for Kelly's and held it lightly in her hands, almost afraid to open it.

What would it be? She had agonized over what to get Kelly. She had wanted to get her something personal, and she had looked for days for the perfect gift. She had finally settled on a gold bracelet with Kelly's name engraved on it. She had planned to give it to her when she got back.

Now, she twisted the gift in her hand, brushing the ribbons with nervous fingers. She glanced up once, but Betsy and Janis were purposely giving her a moment to herself. She was thankful. She tore the wrapping off finally, revealing a black velvet box. Her hands trembled. Opening it slowly, her breath caught. Inside was a delicate gold chain and, dangling from the end, two gold hearts entwined, twin diamonds winking at her, one in each heart. She lifted the necklace out with care and held it in her hands, tears pricking her eyes. There was a note inside that she took out with gentle fingers.

"Our hearts are like this, separate, but one," Kelly had written. "They need the other to be happy and strong. Please accept this and wear it with my love. You hold my heart in your hands."

Jo brought the note to her mouth and let her tears fall. Her heart felt like it would explode. She took deep breaths, trying to stop her tears.

"Jo?"

"I'm okay," she whispered.

And she was. The gift was more than she had expected but it was Kelly's words that touched her. She had been a fool to think Kelly would end up hurting her. Kelly loved her. And Jo loved her back.

She endured another hour, then made her escape.

"You're coming back for dinner, aren't you?" Betsy asked.

"Of course."

She pulled Betsy closer and whispered, "I've just got to call her. And I can't do it here."

"Are you all right?"

"I'm more than all right," Jo said and grinned.

She rushed home, unmindful of traffic laws, and hurried into her house. She found the phone number where Kelly had left it and quickly dialed, unconcerned with what time it might be in California.

"Merry Christmas," a pleasant voice answered.

"Merry Christmas," Jo returned. "I hope I'm not calling too early, but I'm a friend of Kelly's from Austin. Could I please speak with her?"

"Of course. Wait one moment."

Jo's palms were damp, and she rubbed them on her jeans, trying to calm her nerves while she waited for Kelly to pick up. She didn't want to think about why she was calling her, she only knew that she had to.

"Jo?"

"Merry Christmas," she said.

"To you, too."

"Am I calling at a bad time?"

"You could never call at a bad time, honey."

Jo's breath caught and her heart lodged in her throat at the simple endearment. "Kelly, I'm so sorry," she said, and her voice trembled.

"What is it?"

"I opened your gift."

"You didn't like it? Was it too much?"

"No, that's not it at all." She took a deep breath, then continued. "I love you. I love you so much. I'm so sorry," she sobbed.

"Jo, please, don't cry. God, I wish I were there with you," Kelly said quietly.

"I'm sorry," Jo said again. "But I love you."

"Why do you tell me you love me in one breath and you're sorry in the next?" she asked gently.

"Because I couldn't tell you before. Because I've been so very awful to you," she said, wiping the tears from her cheeks absently.

"And you couldn't wait a second longer to tell me?" Kelly asked, and Jo could tell she was smiling.

"No," Jo whispered.

"Honey, you sure can pick your moments."

"I miss you and I couldn't wait another day to tell you that I love you."

"I'll be home tomorrow. Don't pick me up at the airport. I don't want to say hello to you in front of hundreds of people. I'll get a cab."

"Okay. I won't."

"And Jo?"

"Yes?"

"Thank you for calling me. You made my Christmas."

Chapter Thirty

Jo waited patiently by the fire, glancing only occasionally at the clock. Now that Kelly was coming, she was suddenly nervous. There was no going back, not after her phone call yesterday. She fingered the gold chain at her neck and smiled. She didn't want to go back. She had never been so happy, so much in love.

She visibly jumped when she heard the urgent knock at her door, and she made herself walk, not run, to open it.

Kelly stood there, eyes searching Jo's, and she smiled slowly. She, too, looked nervous.

"Oh, God, I missed you," Kelly whispered.

Jo took her hand and pulled her inside, her eyes never leaving Kelly's.

"I missed you, too."

Kelly drew Jo into her arms, and Jo breathed the sweet scent of her that she knew so well. Their lips met, softly, gently, unhurried.

"Tell me," Kelly demanded.

"I love you," Jo said, meeting her eyes. "I've loved you for so long."

Kelly smiled, and Jo thought she saw relief in that smile as she touched Kelly's face with gentle fingers.

"I love you, Jo. I can't imagine my life without you," she whispered.

"Then let's don't," Jo said with a smile. "Because I intend on spending the rest of mine with you."

"I won't hurt you," Kelly promised.

"I know. I'm only sorry it took me so long to figure that out."

Kelly led her into the bedroom, a smile firmly in place.

"You can spend the rest our lives making it up to me," she said.

"It will be my pleasure."

Publications from
BELLA BOOKS, INC.
The best in contemporary lesbian fiction

P.O. Box 10543, Tallahassee, FL 32302
Phone: 800-729-4992
www.bellabooks.com

SUGAR by Karin Kallmaker. 240 pp. Three women want sugar from Sugar, who can't make up her mind. ISBN 1-59493-001-5 $12.95

FALL GUY by Claire McNab. 200 pp. 16th Detective Inspector Carol Ashton Mystery. ISBN 1-59493-000-7 $12.95

ONE SUMMER NIGHT by Gerri Hill. 232 pp. Johanna swore to never fall in love again—but then she met the charming Kelly . . . ISBN 1-59493-007-4 $12.95

TALK OF THE TOWN TOO by Saxon Bennett. 181 pp. Second in the series about wild and fun loving friends. ISBN 1-931513-77-5 $12.95

…E SPEAKS HER NAME by Laura DeHart Young. 170 pp. Love and friendship, desire …ntrigue, spark this exciting sequel to *Forever and the Night.* ISBN 1-59493-002-3 $12.95

… HAVE AND TO HOLD by Peggy J. Herring. 184 pp. By finally letting down her …enses, will Dorian be opening herself to a devastating betrayal? ISBN 1-59493-005-8 $12.95

…ILD THINGS by Karin Kallmaker. 228 pp. Dutiful daughter Faith has met the perfect …an. There's just one problem: she's in love with his sister. ISBN 1-931513-64-3 $12.95

…HARED WINDS by Kenna White. 216 pp. Can Emma rebuild more than just Lanny's …arina? ISBN 1-59493-006-6 $12.95

…HE UNKNOWN MILE by Jaime Clevenger. 253 pp. Kelly's world is getting more and more complicated every moment. ISBN 1-931513-57-0 $12.95

TREASURED PAST by Linda Hill. 189 pp. A shared passion for antiques leads to love. ISBN 1-59493-003-1 $12.95

SIERRA CITY by Gerri Hill. 284 pp. Chris and Jesse cannot deny their growing attraction . . . ISBN 1-931513-98-8 $12.95

ALL THE WRONG PLACES by Karin Kallmaker. 174 pp. Sex and the single girl—Brandy is looking for love and usually she finds it. Karin Kallmaker's first *After Dark* erotic novel. ISBN 1-931513-76-7 $12.95

WHEN THE CORPSE LIES A Motor City Thriller by Therese Szymanski. 328 pp. Butch bad-girl Brett Higgins is used to waking up next to beautiful women she hardly knows. Problem is, this one's dead. ISBN 1-931513-74-0 $12.95

GUARDED HEARTS by Hannah Rickard. 240 pp. Someone's reminding Alyssa about her secret past, and then she becomes the suspect in a series of burglaries.
ISBN 1-931513-99-6 $12.95

ONCE MORE WITH FEELING by Peggy J. Herring. 184 pp. Lighthearted, loving, romantic adventure. ISBN 1-931513-60-0 $12.95

TANGLED AND DARK A Brenda Strange Mystery by Patty G. Henderson. 240 pp. When investigating a local death, Brenda finds two possible killers—one diagnosed with Multiple Personality Disorder. ISBN 1-931513-75-9 $12.95

WHITE LACE AND PROMISES by Peggy J. Herring. 240 pp. Maxine and Betina realize sex may not be the most important thing in their lives. ISBN 1-931513-73-2 $12.95

UNFORGETTABLE by Karin Kallmaker. 288 pp. Can Rett find love with the cheerleader who broke her heart so many years ago? ISBN 1-931513-63-5 $12.95

HIGHER GROUND by Saxon Bennett. 280 pp. A delightfully complex reflection of the successful, high society lives of a small group of women. ISBN 1-931513-69-4 $12.95

LAST CALL A Detective Franco Mystery by Baxter Clare. 240 pp. Frank overlooks all else to try to solve a cold case of two murdered children . . . ISBN 1-931513-70-8 $12.95

ONCE UPON A DYKE: NEW EXPLOITS OF FAIRY-TALE LESBIANS by Karin Kallmaker, Julia Watts, Barbara Johnson & Therese Szymanski. 320 pp. You've never read fairy tales like these before! From Bella After Dark. ISBN 1-931513-71-6 $14.95

FINEST KIND OF LOVE by Diana Tremain Braund. 224 pp. Can Molly and Carolyn stop clashing long enough to see beyond their differences? ISBN 1-931513-68-6 $12.95

DREAM LOVER by Lyn Denison. 188 pp. A soft, sensuous, romantic fantasy.
ISBN 1-931513-96-1 $12.95

NEVER SAY NEVER by Linda Hill. 224 pp. A classic love story . . . where rules aren't the only things broken. ISBN 1-931513-67-8 $12.95

PAINTED MOON by Karin Kallmaker. 214 pp. Stranded together in a snowbound cabin, Jackie and Leah's lives will never be the same. ISBN 1-931513-53-8 $12.95

WIZARD OF ISIS by Jean Stewart. 240 pp. Fifth in the exciting Isis series.
ISBN 1-931513-71-4 $12.95

WOMAN IN THE MIRROR by Jackie Calhoun. 216 pp. Josey learns to love again, while her niece is learning to love women for the first time. ISBN 1-931513-78-3 $12.95

SUBSTITUTE FOR LOVE by Karin Kallmaker. 200 pp. When Holly and Reyna meet the combination adds up to pure passion. But what about tomorrow? ISBN 1-931513-62-7 $12.95

GULF BREEZE by Gerri Hill. 288 pp. Could Carly really be the woman Pat has always been searching for? ISBN 1-931513-97-X $12.95

THE TOMSTOWN INCIDENT by Penny Hayes. 184 pp. Caught between two worlds, Eloise must make a decision that will change her life forever. ISBN 1-931513-56-2 $12.95

MAKING UP FOR LOST TIME by Karin Kallmaker. 240 pp. Discover delicious recipes for romance by the undisputed mistress. ISBN 1-931513-61-9 $12.95

THE WAY LIFE SHOULD BE by Diana Tremain Braund. 173 pp. With which woman will Jennifer find the true meaning of love? ISBN 1-931513-66-X $12.95

BACK TO BASICS: A BUTCH/FEMME ANTHOLOGY edited by Therese Szymanski—from Bella After Dark. 324 pp. ISBN 1-931513-35-X $14.95